The
Crimson Cryptogram
A Detective Story

by

Fergus Hume

The Crimson Cryptogram
A Detective Story
by Fergus Hume

ISBN: 978-93-62205-78-0

Published by

DOUBLE 9 BOOKS

2/13-B, Ansari Road
Daryaganj, New Delhi – 110002
info@double9books.com
www.double9books.com
Tel. 011-40042856

ABOUT THE AUTHOR

Ferguson Wright Hume, also known as Fergus Hume, was a prolific English novelist who wrote detective fiction, thrillers, and mysteries. Hume was born in Powick, Worcestershire, England, as the second son of James C. Hume, a Scot who worked as a clerk and steward at the county pauper and lunatic asylum. When he was three, his family moved to Dunedin, New Zealand, where he attended Otago Boys' High School and studied law at the University of Otago. He was admitted to the New Zealand Bar in 1885. Hume moved to Melbourne, Australia, shortly after graduating and began working as a barristers' clerk. He began writing plays but was unable to persuade Melbourne theatre managers to approve, let alone read them. Hume returned to England, first in London, then in Thundersley, Essex, at Church Cottage, most likely on the invitation of the Reverend Thomas Noon Talfourd Major. Hume resided in Thundersley for thirty years, producing over 130 novels and various collections, the most of which were mystery stories, although he never regained the fame of his debut novel. He also wrote lyrics for songs written by his brother-in-law, Charles Willeby, and book reviews for literary periodicals such as The Bookman. The 1911 census shows him as 'author', aged 51, and living at Church Cottage, Thundersley, which comprised of six rooms. He had a housekeeper, Ada Louise Peck, a widow aged 69. He made regular trips to Italy, France, Switzerland, and other European countries.

CONTENTS

CHAPTER I
A MIDNIGHT SURPRISE

"Poverty, naked and unconcealed! One can endure that, with some patience, as a beaten soldier in the battle of life. But genteel pauperism-- the semi-poverty of the middle-class, that lives a necessary lie at the cost of incessant worry and constant defeat--there you have the true misery of life. Believe me, Cass, there is no torture like that of an ambition which cannot be attained for lack of money."

"I did not know you were ambitious, Ellis."

"Not of setting the Thames on fire. My desires are limited to a good practice, a moderate income, a home, and a wife to love me. These wishes are reasonable enough, Heaven knows, yet some cursed Fate prevents their realisation. And I have to sit down and wait; a doctor can do nothing else. I must listen with such philosophy as I have for the ring of the door bell to announce my first patient, and the ring never comes. The heart grows sick, the brain rusty, the money goes, the temper sours, and so I pass the best days of my life."

"All things come to him who knows how to wait," said Cass, knocking the ashes out of a well-smoked briar.

"And the horse is the noblest of all animals," retorted Ellis. "I never *did* find consolation in proverbs of that class."

The two men sat in their dingy sitting-room talking as usual of a problematical future. Every night they discussed the subject, and every discussion ended without any definite conclusion being arrived at. Indeed, only Fortune could have terminated the arguments in a satisfactory manner, but as yet the fickle deity showed no disposition to make a third in the conversation. Therefore, Robert Ellis, M.D., and Harry Cass, journalist, talked, and talked, and talked. They also hoped for the best, a state of mind sufficiently eloquent of their penniless position. Unless they or their relatives are sick, rich people have no need to hope for the best. The second virtue dwells almost exclusively with the poor and ambitious, as do her two sisters.

Supper was just over, but even cold beef, pickles and bottled beer, with the after comfort of a pipe, could not make Ellis happy. The more philosophical Cass lay on the ragged sofa and digested his meal, while the doctor walked up and down the room railing at Fate. He was a tall young man, clean-limbed, and sufficiently good-looking. Poverty and former opulence showed themselves in the threadbare velveteen smoking suit he wore; and the past recurred to him as he flicked some ash off this relic of bygone days.

"O Lord!" he said regretfully, "how jolly life was when I bought these clothes some five years ago! My father had not died a bankrupt country squire then; and I was a rowdy medico, with plenty of money, and a weakness for the other sex."

"You haven't strengthened in that direction, Bob."

"Perhaps not; but I never think of women now--not even of a possible wife. Matrimony is a luxury a poor man must dispense with, if he wants to get on. I have dispensed with every blessed thing short of the bare necessities of existence, yet I don't get any reward. Every dog has his day, they say: but the day of this poor cur never seems to dawn."

"You are more bitter than usual, Ellis."

"Because I am sick of my life. You have some compensations, Harry, in connection with that newspaper you write for. You mix with your fellow-men; you exchange ideas; you have your finger on the pulse of civilisation. But I sit in this dismal room, or walk about this B[oe]otian neighbourhood, in the vain hope of getting a start. I can't rush out and drag in someone to be dosed; I can't go from house to house soliciting patients. I can only wait wait, wait; until I feel inclined to blow my brains out."

"If you did that, Bob, the folly of the act would prove that you have none," said Cass. "Come, old man, buck up; something is sure to turn up when you least expect it."

"Then nothing will turn up, for I am always in a state of expectation. I wish I hadn't set up my tent at Dukesfield, Harry. It is the healthiest London suburb I know: no one seems ill, and the graveyard is almost empty. I don't believe people ever fall sick or die in this salubrious spot."

Cass ran his fingers through a shock of bronze-coloured hair, and laughed at this professional view of the situation. "Haven't you seen any likely patient?" he asked, in his most sympathetic manner.

"Not one!" rejoined Ellis, sitting down and relighting his pipe. "Oh, yes, by the way, that young Moxton."

"Who the deuce is he?"

"A young ass I have met several times in the underground train, and with whom I have had some conversation at various times."

"Why do you call him an ass?"

"Because he is one," growled the doctor; "he is burning the candle at both ends, and killing himself with dissipation. Tallow face, blood-shot eyes, dry lips. Oh, Mr. Moxton is making for the graveyard at racing speed!"

"Why don't you warn him?"

"It isn't my business to meddle with a stranger. I don't care if he lives or dies--unless he takes me as his medical attendant. Even then my interest in him would be purely professional. He is a detestable young cub."

"There is a want of pity about that speech, Bob!"

"Want of money, you mean. I have no pity for anyone save mine own poor self. Give me success, give me an income, and I'll overflow with the milk of human kindness. Poverty and disappointment is drying it all up. Hullo! Come in, Mrs. Basket."

This invitation was induced, not by a rap at the door, but by the sound of stertorous breathing outside it. Mrs. Basket's coming was audible long before she made her appearance; so Ellis, forewarned, usually saved her the trouble of knocking. She rolled heavily into the room, labouring like a Dutch lugger in a heavy sea. Indeed, she was built on similar lines, being squat and enormously stout--so bulky, indeed, that she could hardly push herself through the door. Like most fat women, Mrs. Basket had a weakness for bright colours; and now presented herself in a vividly blue dress, a crimson shawl, and a green tulle cap decorated with buttercups of an aggressive yellow hue. Her unshapely figure, her large proportions and barbaric splendour, would have made the eyes and heart of an artist ache; but as Mrs. Basket's lodgers knew little of art, they never troubled about her looks. Moreover, they liked and respected her as a kindly soul, for on several occasions, when funds were low, she had pressed neither of them for rent. Mrs. Basket was immensely proud of having a medical man under her roof; and always personally polished the brass plate with "Robert Ellis, M.D.," inscribed on it. For Cass she had less respect, as being merely a "writing person;" but she tolerated him as the doctor's friend. Like the moon, he shone with a reflected and weaker glory.

"Lor', gentlemen, how them stairs do try me!" said the good lady, panting in the doorway and patting her ample breast; "they're that steep and that narrer, as to squeeze the breath out of me."

"You'll stick halfway up some day!" said Cass, chuckling, "then we shall have to send for a carpenter to saw you out!"

Mrs. Basket laughed, in nowise offended, and announced that she had come to clear away supper, which she did with much clatter and hard breathing. Once or twice she glanced at the doctor's gloomy face, and blew a sigh with considerable noise. She knew of her lodger's bad fortune, and pitied him profoundly; but not daring to speak, she resumed her work with a mournful wag of the buttercup cap. Ignoring this by-play, which invited conversation, the young men resumed the subject of Moxton. Mrs. Basket, dying to join in, at once espied an opportunity of doing so. The mere mention of the name was enough to set her off.

"Lor', gentlemen, you do turn me cold to my bones. Moxton! Why, the name makes me shiver," and Mrs. Basket shivered duly to prove the truth of her words.

Usually the lodgers did not encourage their landlady to talk, as her tongue, once set wagging, was difficult to stop. But on this occasion her speech was so significant of mystery that Ellis wheeled round his chair to face her, and the reporter on the sofa, with true journalistic instinct, was at once on the alert for news. Mrs. Basket, pleased with these tokens of interest, improved upon her speech.

"He has a wife!" said she, and closed her eyes with another shiver.

"Is that a remarkable circumstance?" asked Cass, drily.

"P'r'aps not, sir," replied Mrs. Basket, with great dignity. "But what that pore young thing suffers the butcher and the baker do know."

"Does Moxton ill-treat her?"

"'Eaven only knows what he do do, doctor. Nobody's ever seen her save the telegraph boy as called after dark, to be met with a carving-knife."

"A carving-knife! This is interesting. Who had the carving-knife, Mrs. Basket?"

"Mrs. Moxton, of course. She is young and pretty, I do assure you, gentlemen, yet she came on the child with a knife in her 'and like Lady Macbeth in the play."

"What was that for?"

Mrs. Basket wagged her head and the buttercups responded. "She told the boy as she thought he was robbers, and came out with the wepping to protect the silver. But it looks like loonatics to me."

"Do you mean to say she is mad?"

"Doctor, I says nothing, being above scandal, But this I do say, as she ought to be mad if she ain't. That Moxton"--Mrs. Basket shivered like a jelly--"goes out night after night, leaving her shut up in that lonely 'ouse."

"Is the house lonely?"

"Mr. Cass, I won't deceive you. It's that lonely as graveyards is company to it. Myrtle Viller they calls it, and it's the larst 'ouse of the row as is spreading out in the brickfield direction. The other villers are unfinished, the contractor as was building them 'aving died with only Myrtle Viller ready to move into. His relatives is a-quarrelling so over his money as they've let the villers be for six months. Mr. and Mrs. Moxton took up 'ouse in the larst of 'em three months come next week, and they're the only pair as lives in that 'orrible lonely road."

As Mrs. Basket drew breath after this long speech and lifted the tray, Ellis put a leading question: "Don't they keep a servant?"

"No, they don't, sir, not as much as a work'us orfan. She is all alone in the 'ouse night after night, as I tells you, and it ain't no wonder as she keeps the carving-knife 'andy."

"Where does Moxton go so regularly?"

"Ah, Mr. Cass, where indeed? P'r'aps the perlice may know."

"Come now, Mrs. Basket, you have no ground for making such a statement."

"Oh, 'aven't I?" cried Mrs. Basket, indignantly. "Why, he's well orf and passes his days indoors doing nothing. 'Ow then does he earn his money? Why does he leave her alone? What's she doing with no servant and a carving-knife? No grounds!" Mrs. Basket waddled towards the door, nose in air, and paused there to deliver a last word: "I shouldn't be surprised at 'earing of a tragedy between 'em. Oh, that dratted bell! And at half-past eleven, too! Decent folk should be a-bed."

The night-bell of Ellis's was ringing furiously, and Mrs. Basket, putting down the tray, squeezed through the door as hurriedly as her unwieldy form permitted. As the tail of her blue skirt whisked out of sight, Cass jumped up from the sofa and smote the doctor's shoulder.

"Here is your first patient, Bob. Fortune is knocking at the door!"

"Ringing, you mean," said Ellis, joking, to hide his agitation.

As he spoke, the voice of Mrs. Basket was heard in wordy expostulation, and a light-footed visitor flitted along the passage and into the room. The new-comer proved to be a woman, young and pretty, bareheaded, and apparently wild with terror. Her entrance and appearance were dramatic.

"The doctor!" she gasped, leaning against the door-post to support her trembling limbs.

"I am a doctor," said Ellis, advancing. "What is it?"

"My husband--my husband is--dead!" She paused with a catching in the throat, then her voice leaped to alto: "Murdered!"

"Murdered!" exclaimed both men, with a simultaneous movement forward.

"Murdered, in the garden! Doctor, come! come!"

"Who is your husband?" stammered Ellis, his wits not quite under control. "What is his name?"

"Moxton! Moxton!" she answered impatiently. "Come, doctor, don't lose time! I am Mrs. Moxton. My husband has been murdered!"

CHAPTER II
THE WRITING IN BLOOD

The long arm of coincidence was startlingly apparent in this instance. Both men were so amazed at the terrible news fitting in so neatly, not only with the subject of conversation, but with Mrs. Basket's prophetic remark when the bell rang, that they looked at one another dumbfounded. Mrs. Moxton stared at their motionless figures with indignant eyes.

"Are you not coming?" she demanded vehemently, seizing the hand of Ellis. "Don't I tell you my husband is dead!"

"I am coming, Mrs. Moxton," said Ellis, hurriedly. "But if he is dead my presence will be useless. This is a case for the police."

If Mrs. Moxton was pale before she became even paler at this last remark, and, shrinking back, spread out her hands with a terrified gesture. "No, no, not the police! Why the police?"

"You say your husband has been murdered," cried Cass, with sudden suspicion; "therefore the police must be called in at once. Who murdered the man?"

"I don't know," murmured Mrs. Moxton. Then his imperious, suspicious tone seemed to stir her indignation. She threw back her head haughtily. "I don't know," she repeated deliberately. "My husband went out this evening. I sat up for him as he promised to return about midnight. Shortly after eleven"--here she glanced at the clock on the mantelpiece--"I heard a cry, and thinking something was wrong I ran to the door. There was someone moaning on the garden path. I went to see who it was, and found my husband bleeding to death from a wound in the back. He died a minute afterwards, and I came for you."

"How did you recognise your husband in the dark?"

"I--I had a candle," she replied, in a low voice and with hesitation.

"It's blowing awful," wheezed Mrs. Basket at the door, and the other woman turned towards her abruptly. The landlady's full moon of a face had suspicion written in every wrinkle. "Had you the carving-knife?" she asked.

"The carving-knife?"

"Yes, the same as you frightened the telegraph boy with?"

"I had no carving-knife," returned Mrs. Moxton, haughtily. "What do you mean by these questions?" She turned again to the men and burst into furious speech. "Have I come to a lunatic asylum?" she cried. "You talk, this woman talks, and I want help. Doctor, come! Come at once! And you, sir, go for the police if it is necessary."

Ellis hastily threw on a cap, snatched up some needful things for a wounded man, and followed Mrs. Moxton out of the house. Mrs. Basket and Harry were left face to face with the same thought in their minds.

"What did I say about her 'aving the carving-knife, sir?"

"Yes, by Jove! And her talking of exploring with a lighted candle in this wind!"

"She's afraid of the police, too, Mr. Cass," said Mrs. Basket, in tragic tones. "She's done for him, sir."

"Well--she--might--No," cried Harry, rumpling his hair. "If she was guilty she would not come for Ellis."

Mrs. Basket snorted in a disbelieving manner.

"Oh, wouldn't she, sir? You don't know the hussies women are. That Mrs. Moxton's a deep 'un as ever was."

"Here," cried Cass, rummaging about for his cap, "I'm losing time. I must go for the police at once."

"Come back and tell me if they takes her," shouted Mrs. Basket after him with morbid glee. "I believe she's done it with the carving-knife."

But Cass did not hear her, as the wind was high and he was already some distance away. As he sped along the silent streets storm-clouds were racing across the face of a watery moon, and a drizzle of rain moistened his face. Being a reporter, Cass was friendly with constables, and knew the station at Dukesfield well, having often gone there to glean paragraphs. This time he went to give more terrible and sensational news than he had ever received, and stumbled almost into Inspector Drake's arms in his haste.

"Steady there," said Drake, gruffly, then recognising the agitated face of Cass in the flaring gaslight, he added, in a tone of surprise: "You, sir; whatever's come over you at this time of night?"

"Drake, there has been a murder at Myrtle Villa down the Jubilee Road, leading to the brickfields. A man called Moxton has been stabbed. His wife came for Dr. Ellis, and I ran on to tell you!"

The inspector heard this startling intelligence with a phlegm begotten by twenty years' experience of similar reports. "Who done it, Mr. Cass? Does the wife know?"

"No; she says she heard a cry, and ran out to find her husband dying on the garden path. He died in her arms."

"Did she see anyone about?"

"I don't know. I never asked her. That is your business, Drake. Come along, Ellis is with her and the dead man."

"Oh, he is dead, then?" remarked the inspector, leisurely putting on his cap and cloak.

"So Mrs. Moxton says. Come!"

Leaving the station in charge of an underling, Drake called a policeman, and followed Cass into the windy night. The two, with the constable tailing after them, marched military fashion along several deserted and lampless streets, until they turned into the Jubilee Road, a dark thoroughfare of empty, roofless houses and incomplete pavements. Civilisation had not yet established order in this region, and the street in embryo ended suddenly on the verge of naked lands. Beyond twinkled the red and green signal lights of the railway, and between, piles of bricks were heaped in Babylon-like mounds. Myrtle Villa was the last house on the right abutting on this untrimmed plain; and the three men were guided to it by a winking light in the garden. It was that of a lantern held by Mrs. Moxton, and shed yellow rays on the face of the dead man. Ellis, kneeling beside the corpse, completed a startling and dramatic picture.

"Oh!" cried the woman, with something like dismay, as the light revealed uniforms, "the police!"

"Yes, ma'am," said Drake, glancing sharply at her white cheeks, "we have come to see about this matter. Is the gentleman dead, doctor?"

"I should think so. Look here!" Ellis rolled over the body and showed a wound under the left shoulder-blade, round which the blood had coagulated. "The poor devil must have died within ten minutes after the blow was struck."

"He died in my arms," moaned Mrs. Moxton. "Oh, Edgar!"

"Did he tell you who stabbed him, ma'am?"

"No; he never spoke a word."

The inspector took the lantern from her shaking hand, and swung it round between corpse and gate. The path was of beaten gravel, and no footmarks were visible; but here and there a stain of blood soaked into the ground, and from this Drake drew his conclusions.

"He was stabbed from behind while opening the gate," he said judicially, "and fell forward into the garden. Look at this stain, and this; the poor gentleman had strength enough to crawl these few yards. Wanted to reach the door, no doubt. What brought you out, ma'am?"

"His cry! I was waiting up for him in the back bedroom, and I heard a shriek. At first I was afraid, as this place is very lonely. Then I came to the door with a candle, and ran down the path. Edgar was moaning dreadfully, and died almost immediately afterwards."

"The wind is high, ma'am?"

Mrs. Moxton understood his inference directly. "It blew out the candle," she explained; "but I ran from the door, shading it with my hand, and as there was a lull for a moment, I had just time to catch a glimpse of his face and recognise my husband."

"About what time was this, ma'am?"

"Some time after eleven. I can't say when. I did not look at my watch."

"It was exactly half-past eleven when you entered my house," said Ellis.

"Then Edgar was murdered between eleven and half-past. I wound up my watch for the night at eleven, and at that time I had not heard the cry. I ran all the way to your house."

"That would take five minutes, more or less," said Cass.

"And the man must have lived some minutes after the blow, to crawl this distance," observed the inspector, measuring the space with his eye. "Did you come out at once, ma'am?"

"No!" replied Mrs. Moxton, with some hesitation. "I was afraid. I heard the cry and waited for a time, thinking I was mistaken. It was about ten minutes, more or less, before I summoned up courage to open the front door."

"On the whole," said Ellis, "it would seem that the murder was committed at a quarter past eleven. Well, Mr. Drake, what is to be done?"

"Nothing can be done until the morning," replied Drake. "The man who did this is no doubt far enough away by this time."

"A man!" cried Mrs. Moxton. "Do you think a man did it?"

The inspector was on the alert immediately. "Have you any reason to think that a woman killed him?" he asked sharply.

"I! No. I cannot guess who committed the murder." Mrs. Moxton seemed anxious, nervous, and sorry she had said so much. "Shall we take the body into the house, sir?" she asked in a low tone.

"It will be as well, ma'am, and I shall leave this constable to look after it for the night."

"Thank you, thank you," said the widow, shuddering. "I should be afraid to stay by myself."

"Let me stay also!" said Ellis, moved by her beauty and distress.

"Oh, do, do. Would you mind?"

"I'll stay," replied the doctor, briefly, and assisted the others to lift the body. They carried it up the path, Mrs. Moxton lighting them onward with the lantern. It was a strange and gruesome procession pacing through the black and stormy night; and to imaginative Cass the house and garden, commonplace as they were, reeked of the shambles.

When the body was laid on the bed, Drake gave some directions to his subordinate, and departed with Cass. Ellis and the policeman remained behind, and the doctor's first care was to give Mrs. Moxton a bromide tabloid.

"You are worn out with anxiety and nerves," he said. "I saw that at my house, and so brought these tabloids with me. Lie down and sleep."

"Shall I ever sleep again?" sighed Mrs. Moxton. However, she obediently did as she was told, and then the men turned their attention to the corpse.

It was that of a lean young man with scanty light hair, and a thin, fair moustache. The lines of dissipation, the marks of premature ageing from debauchery, had been smoothed out by death, and the white face was as unwrinkled and placid as a waxen mask. The body was clothed in evening dress, with a light-coloured overcoat, and the constable pointed out to Ellis that the watch, chain, studs and links--all costly--were untouched.

"Robbers didn't bring about this murder," said the policeman.

They undressed the body slowly. As Ellis drew off the shirt, the cuffs of which were dappled with blood, he noticed strange marks on the left arm. From wrist to elbow, on the inner part of the arm, various signs appeared on the white skin. These were rudely streaked with blood, and Ellis afterwards copied them into his note-book, thinking they might be useful later on, as indeed they proved to be.

"What do these signs mean?" he asked the policeman.

"I dunno, sir; but he did 'em hisself. See, doctor," and he lifted the right hand of the corpse.

Ellis looked eagerly and saw that the forefinger of the hand was black with dried blood.

CHAPTER III
AN OPEN VERDICT

Next day the body of the unfortunate man was removed to the Dukesfield morgue, and twenty-four hours later the coroner held an inquiry in the coffee-room of the Lancaster Hotel. Public interest was greatly roused over the matter, and the ubiquitous reporters of the great "dailies"--amongst them Harry Cass--attended, note-book in hand, to supply their readers with sensational details. A rumour--first set afloat by the babbling tongue of Mrs. Basket--was prevalent that Mrs. Moxton had killed her husband with a carving-knife. It was known from the same source that she had lived a lonely life since taking up her abode in Myrtle Villa, that Moxton had neglected her shamefully, that he had left her nightly by herself, and had even denied her the comfort and company of a servant. Hence it was openly declared that cruel treatment and contemptuous desertion had driven Mrs. Moxton to commit the crime. But this theory found no favour in the sight of Dr. Ellis, and he avowed himself the champion of the pretty widow.

"If she were guilty she would not have announced the crime as she did," he argued with Cass. "It would have been easy for her to let the corpse lie on the path all night, and pretend ignorance when it was discovered by the milkman. Also, if she struck the blow she had a whole night at her disposal to vanish into the unknown."

"Flight would have proved her guilt, Bob. Besides, she would have been tracked down on that tacit confession of her crime."

"I don't agree with you. Nothing is known of the Moxtons, as they kept very much to themselves. Hardly anyone saw her or knew her by sight. She could have disappeared like a drop of water into the ocean of London, without leaving a trace for the most cunning detective to follow. Instead of doing this--her wisest plan if she killed her husband--she stays and faces the matter out in all innocence."

Cass produced a newspaper from his pocket. "I can suggest a theory for her remaining. Here"--he pointed to a paragraph in the death column--"three days ago, Edgar Allan Moxton, the great picture-dealer of Bond Street, died, leaving a large fortune behind him. Now this dead man, as I judge from the similarity of Christian and surname, is probably the son of Moxton. If so, he, had he lived, would, no doubt, inherit the money. As he is dead, Mrs. Moxton, the widow, may do so. A fortune is worth running some risk for, Bob."

But the faith of Ellis was not to be shaken.

"The similarity of names may be a mere coincidence, such as occurs more frequently in real life than in fiction. Also, even if you can prove the relationship, it does not show that Mrs. Moxton is waiting for the fortune, or that she is even aware of the death. Give her the benefit of the doubt, Harry."

"I give her much more than the jury will do, Ellis. Public opinion is against her."

"Bah! what do the tinker and tailor and candlestick maker know of the matter?"

"They may not know much now, but they will soon be primed with sufficient evidence to give a verdict. The jury is chosen from the class you mention so contemptuously."

Dr. Ellis knew this very well, and knew, moreover, that rumour spoke ill of the widow. Therefore, it was with some doubt whether she would have a fair hearing that he attended the inquest. By the time he arrived the hotel was so crowded that the people overflowed into the road. The young man pushed his way into the public room and found that the proceedings had already commenced. He glanced round for Mrs. Moxton, and saw her seated near the coroner, clothed in black, closely veiled, and listening attentively to Drake's evidence.

The inspector's testimony was brief and meagre, for the police had, as yet, discovered nothing. He described the finding of the body, the futile search for the weapon with which the murder had been committed, and the failure of his attempt to learn where the deceased had so regularly spent his nights. Nevertheless, the identity of the dead man had been established, for he was the son of a Bond Street picture-dealer, Edgar Allan Moxton. Strange to say, father and son had died within a few hours of one another, the former in the morning from natural causes, the latter shortly before midnight by violence. Finally, Drake stated that hitherto the police had found no clue likely to lead to the identification and capture of the murderer.

"Which shows that the police don't suspect Mrs. Moxton," murmured Ellis to Cass.

The doctor himself was the next witness, and deposed as to his summons by Mrs. Moxton, and his examination of the corpse. Deceased had died from the stab of a broad-bladed knife which had pierced the left lung. The blow must have been struck by a strong arm, he averred, since the blade had penetrated through an overcoat, inside coat, waistcoat and shirt.

"Could a woman have struck such a blow?" asked one of the jury.

"An exceptionally strong woman might have done so," responded Ellis.

All eyes were turned on the trim, slight figure of Mrs. Moxton, and there was a general feeling that the doctor's answer exonerated her from having personally committed the murder. She was of too frail and delicate a physique to have struck home the knife with so sure and deadly an aim. Yet she might have put the weapon into another's hand, for it seemed incredible that she should be ignorant of the tragedy which took place within a few yards of her. When Mrs. Moxton's name was called out, and she stood up to give evidence, those present drew a long breath and waited eagerly for her to speak. Hitherto public curiosity had been languid; now the appearance of the principal witness stimulated it to fever heat. From the dead man's widow, if from anyone, the truth of this strange tragedy should come.

Mrs. Moxton threw back her veil when she took the oath, and revealed a pretty face, somewhat marred by sleeplessness and weeping. She was colourless, red-eyed and low-voiced, but gathering courage as she proceeded, told her tale with great simplicity and apparent truth. The evidence she gave may be condensed as follows:--

"My name is Laura Moxton. I married my husband, Edgar, twelve months ago. He was the son of Mr. Moxton, of Bond Street, and the heir to great wealth. When he met me I was earning my living by typewriting, and although I refused twice to marry him he insisted that I should do so. At last I yielded and became his wife, whereupon his father cut him off with a shilling. Edgar had some money inherited from his mother, and with this we went to Monte Carlo, where he tried to increase his fortune by gambling. However, he was unlucky, and we returned to London in eight months poorer than when we left. For the sake of economy my husband took Myrtle Villa, as he obtained it at a low rental on account of the unfinished state of the road. For the same reason we dispensed with a servant and hired the furniture. I did all the housework, and for want of money rarely went outside the house. My husband was unkind and neglectful, and accused me of being the cause of the quarrel with his father which had cost him his inheritance. It is now three months since we took Myrtle Villa. My husband, for the first week, remained indoors at night; afterwards he went out regularly. I did not know what he did with himself, or where he went, as he always refused to tell me, and his temper became so morose that I was afraid to insist upon his confidence. He always dressed himself carefully in evening dress, and usually wore a light overcoat. As a rule, he returned shortly after midnight. Sometimes I waited up for him, at other times I went to bed. I was often afraid during the long evenings in the house, as it was so lonely and so near the waste lands where the brickworks stand. On the night of the murder my husband went out as usual. It was August 16th. I waited for his return and shut myself up in the bedroom at the back of the house. About eleven I grew tired of waiting and prepared to go to bed. I know it was eleven as I wound up my watch at that hour. I was brushing my hair when I thought I heard a cry, but as the wind was blowing strongly I fancied I was mistaken. Still, the belief was so strong that, after doing up my hair, I took the candle and went to the door. The light showed me someone lying on the path, halfway to the gate I also heard a moan. At once I ran down, shading the candle light in the hollow of my hand. For the moment there was a lull in the wind, and the light burnt long enough to show me that my husband was lying wounded on the path. Then the wind extinguished the light. I took my husband in my arms. He moaned feebly, but could not speak. Then he gave a gasp and died. I was dreadfully afraid, and without waiting to get my hat or cloak, I ran for Dr. Ellis. I saw no one; I heard no one; and I do not know who killed my husband."

"In what position was he lying when you came upon him?"

"On his back. As the light of my candle fell for a moment on his face, I recognised him at once."

"How did you know he was wounded, seeing that the wound was in his back?"

"I saw blood on his shirt-front and coat. Also, his face was so white and he moaned so much that I guessed he was hurt. When I took him in my arms I felt on my fingers the blood flowing from his back."

"Had your husband enemies?"

"I do not know. He introduced me to no one he knew. I lived a lonely life. All the time I was at Myrtle Villa I saw no one but my husband."

"Did you know any of his friends abroad?"

"No. He introduced me to no one."

"Did he ever speak of anyone as having a grudge against him?"

"No. He spoke of himself and his father, but of no one else."

"Did he know that his father was dead when he left the house on August 16th?"

"Not to my knowledge. He said nothing to me. Until I heard Mr. Drake's evidence I did not know myself that Mr. Moxton, senior, was dead."

"Did your husband receive any letter on the day of his death?"

"No. He never received letters, nor did he take in a newspaper. We lived quite isolated from the world. I did not like my position, but I feared to complain, on account of my husband's temper."

"Was your husband's temper such as would provoke enmity?"

"I think so: he had a very bad temper."

"Did he drink much?"

"Yes, he drank a great deal of brandy, and was very morose when intoxicated. When I saw him like that, I used to shut myself in the back bedroom."

"Did your husband treat you cruelly?"

"He neglected me and spoke harshly to me, but he never struck me."

"What were your feelings towards him?"

"I loved him when we married, for then he was kind and good. Afterwards I had no feeling towards him save one of terror."

"On one occasion it is reported that you came to meet a telegraph boy with a carving-knife. Is that true?"

"Perfectly true. But I did not know who was at the door. It was growing dark, and the house was very lonely. I took the knife in case it might be a tramp."

"Did you usually carry the knife to protect yourself?"

"Oh, no! On that occasion I was in the kitchen, and snatched it from the table when the knock came to the door."

"You never went to the door with it on any other occasion?"

"Certainly not. No one else ever came after dark. The tradespeople called always in the daytime. Then I was not afraid."

"For whom was the telegram?"

"For my husband. I did not open it, but left it on the table in the dining-room. He got it when he came home that night."

"Did he tell you what it was about?"

"No. He never mentioned the subject."

"Do you know anything about the marks in blood on the arm?"

"No. I was shown them by Doctor Ellis, but I do not know what they mean, or, indeed, what they are."

"Do they not look to you like secret writing? Like a cryptogram?"

"I don't know anything about secret writing. They look like blood smears to me. I do not understand them."

"Have you any idea why deceased wrote them on his arm?"

"Not the least in the world."

"Did you ever see your husband use a cypher of that kind?"

"Never. I never saw him use a cypher of any sort."

"Did you ever notice marks like them before?"

"No. I know nothing about them."

"Can you throw any light at all on this murder?"

"None whatever. I was amazed to find my husband dying."

"He said no word--no name?"

"He did nothing but moan, and died in a few moments."

This examination, which lasted some considerable time, concluded all available evidence for the time being. On the meagre intelligence to be gleaned from it the jury framed their verdict, and stated that the deceased, Edgar Moxton, had been murdered by some person or persons unknown.

CHAPTER IV
THE READING OF THE BLOOD SIGNS

In these progressive times, the duration of proverbial wonderment has been reduced from nine days to nine hours. The Dukesfield murder case was mysterious and dramatic, yet, even with these elements of popularity, it became stale and out of date within the week. The attention of the masses and the classes was more or less concentrated on the visit of an Eastern potentate, whose amazing jewels, and still more amazing barbarisms, appealed to the popular humour. Moxton's death and the strange circumstances attendant thereon ceased to be commented upon by the newspapers; they faded out of the public mind, and continued to be talked about only in the neighbourhood wherein the tragedy occurred. Yet even in Dukesfield, after a fortnight of discussion, the interest grew languid.

It was just as well for Mrs. Moxton that circumstances stood thus, for, in defiance of public opinion, she still continued to inhabit Myrtle Villa. Her husband's maltreated body was quietly buried in the Dukesfield cemetery, so quietly, indeed, that, save the necessary undertaker and his men, not a single person followed the unfortunate victim to his untimely grave. It is only justice to say that Mrs. Moxton would have done so but for the earnest advice of Ellis. Knowing her unpopularity and its cause, he warned her against thrusting herself forward. Like a wise woman, the widow took the hint, but passionately resented the reason for which it was given. When the ceremony was at an end, Ellis came to tell her about it, and she defended herself to him after the fashion of women, with many words and much indignation. As soon as he could obtain a hearing, the doctor assured her that in his case such arguments were needless.

"I am a firm believer in your innocence, Mrs. Moxton," he declared, in all earnestness, "and you must not trouble about the idle gossip of the neighbourhood. People will talk, and it is just a chance that they did not call you a martyr instead of a criminal."

"It is shameful that a friendless woman should be so abused!"

"You are not altogether friendless, Mrs. Moxton. If you will accept me as your champion, I shall be proud to occupy the position."

The widow looked steadfastly at Ellis, and something--perceptible to a woman only--which she saw in his eyes caused her to lower her own. She replied indirectly, with true feminine evasion,--

"I shall always be glad to have you for a friend, doctor. You have been--you are--very good to me."

But after this speech Mrs. Moxton became reserved and hesitating, finally silent; so that Ellis, aware that his eyes had revealed too much, took his leave in a few minutes. By this time he was conscious that he had fallen in love with the pretty widow, and marvelled that he should lose his heart after three weeks' acquaintance. In the opinion of some, love at first sight is a fallacy, and at one time Ellis had been of these wiseacres. Now his personal experience proved the truth of the saying. Mrs. Moxton was not a supremely beautiful woman, but she had a young and comely face, and an extraordinarily fascinating manner. It was to this last that Ellis succumbed, and he made scarcely any effort to resist its influence. Yet Mrs. Moxton was a woman with a humble--if not a doubtful--past, and there was a slur on her reputation as the widow of a murdered man. Ellis could not help admitting to himself that she was no wife for a struggling doctor, yet, in spite of such admission, he was bent upon marrying her, should the opportunity offer itself. In the meantime he kept his own counsel and told no one--not even Cass--of this new element in his life.

That same evening Ellis and his friend sat down after supper to discuss again their domestic affairs and the state of the exchequer. The outlook was now considerably improved, for Cass had returned with a good piece of news, which he lost no time in imparting to the doctor.

"The gods of things-as-they-ought-to-be have awakened to the injustice of my terrestrial treatment, Bob," he announced gleefully. "I have been made theatrical critic for the *Early Bird*, and a story of mine has been accepted by the *Piccadilly Magazine*."

"Good news, old boy; I congratulate you. What is the reason for this sudden discovery of your merits?"

"Moxton's murder, I think. My editor was pleased with the blood-and-thunder report I gave of it."

"Hence he sets you to criticise the drama," said Ellis, drily.

"I suppose so. Perhaps he thinks that if I can describe the murder of a human being I can deal with the slaughter of drama and comedy by incompetent actors."

"The profession would be flattered by your preconceived ideas of their capabilities, Harry."

"Nonsense! I am thinking of extreme cases only. But now that I have a better salary I can help you, Bob. I shall be like the Auvergnat carrier in Balzac's story, and aid a great physician to reach his rightful position for the benefit of humanity."

"Thank you, Harry, but I fear I am not sufficiently gifted to deserve your self-denial. Besides, I have been discovered also."

"What? You have a patient?"

"Yes, a morbid lady with nerves. She saw my name in connection with the discovery of that poor devil's body, and came to see me about her own trouble."

"Nerves and murder. I don't see the connection."

"She did, however," said Ellis, with a shrug, "and asked me to save her life. It is in no danger, as you may guess. She is nothing but an excitable female with too much money and no employment. I wrote her a prescription, humoured her hypochondria, and so pleased her that she departed, pronouncing me to be a charming young man who thoroughly understood her 'system.' She intends to send all her friends to me."

"That's capital," cried Cass, shaking hands with his friend. "Once you get the start you will soon roll on to fame and fortune. I'll meet you on Tom Tiddler's ground, Bob, and we'll pick up the gold and silver in company. Dr. Robert Ellis, of Harley Street, specialist in eye diseases, and Henry Cass, the great, the only novelist! But I say, Bob," added the journalist, "don't degenerate into a humbug, old man."

"My dear fellow, in dealing with women, one must be a humbug more or less. They like it."

"That is true in every case. Women always prefer the graceful humbugs of this world to the genuine, honest creatures. That is why I have not been snapped up by a rich heiress."

Ellis laughed absently, being more taken up with his own thoughts than with the humour of his friend. "Yes, I believe this patient will send me others, and that, sooner or later, I shall scrape together a practice in Dukesfield. In years to come I may even be able to set up as an eye specialist."

"In Harley Street, Bob, in Harley Street."

"In any street so long as I can make a good income. When I become known as an authority on diseases of the eye----"

"You are known, Bob," interrupted Cass, vigorously. "That book on the eye you wrote is well known."

"Stuff! My book fell still-born from the Press. Besides, if it is known, only my medical brethren have the knowledge. I wish to be popular with the masses, Harry, to have a name with them, for it is the public who pay."

"Well, well, that will come. I believe in your future, Bob. You will have all you wish for--an income, a name, and a wife."

"A wife!" Ellis turned restlessly in the comfortable old arm-chair, and laughed in a somewhat embarrassed fashion. "A wife!" he repeated doubtfully.

"Of course; you don't intend to remain single all your days, do you? You must marry, Bob, for a doctor without a wife, a tactful wife, mind you, is like a coach without wheels. I hope, however," and here Harry's tone became serious, "that you will not marry a widow."

"A widow! I don't quite understand."

"Or," continued Cass, inattentive to the interpolation, "or the wife of a man who has met with a violent death."

"Harry, what makes you think that Mrs. Moxton--" So far Ellis proceeded violently, then stopped with the conviction that he had betrayed his secret.

"The cap fits, I see," remarked Cass, pointedly, and shut up in his turn.

For the next few minutes there was an embarrassed silence, neither man being willing to speak, lest a word should act like a spark in a powder magazine. Ellis threw down his pipe, and, as was his fashion when annoyed, took to rapid walking in the limited space of the sitting-room. Cass eased his position on the sofa and waited developments.

"Yes, it is true," said the doctor, in a loud voice, so as to drown opposition. "I am in love with Mrs. Moxton. Now, what do you say?"

"Only this. It is hard enough for you to make a career without seeking for a clog which will prevent you rising in your profession."

"How do you know Mrs. Moxton would prove such a clog?"

"I don't know; I surmise only. I am ignorant of the lady's personality, save from what I have learnt in chance moments. You are in the like position."

"I know her better than you do."

"Possibly. But do you know her well enough to risk making her your wife?"

"I didn't say that I intended to ask her to marry me."

Cass laughed. "That is a quibble. With honourable men a declared passion is always the prelude to marriage."

"But I have not declared my passion," argued Ellis, in vexed tones.

"Not yet, maybe, but you will do so when the time comes."

"After all, Harry, she is a charming woman."

"Charming and pretty, no doubt. But is she the wife for you? Before you can answer that question, you must know her past and whitewash her present."

Dr. Ellis sat down aghast. "Good heavens, Cass! Surely you don't think her guilty?"

"I don't know enough about the case to say," said Cass, meditatively; "but Mrs. Moxton puzzles me, I confess. For instance, she tells lies."

"Tells lies!" repeated the widow's champion, with great indignation.

"Yes, and in the most unblushing manner. At the inquest she said that she took her husband's body in her arms and felt the blood flowing from the wound in his back. Now, it is my impression that she never touched the body."

"How can you prove that?"

"Very simply. When she came into this room she wore a plain black dress, with cuffs of white linen. Now, if she had handled the body and had touched the wound, it is only natural to suppose that those cuffs would be stained with blood. I noticed, however, that they were not."

"But that is all the stronger proof that she is innocent."

"Of the actual murder, maybe, Bob; but it does not prove that she is ignorant of who killed the man. She told lies about the handling of the body, as I said. It seems to me," added Cass, reflectively, "that Mrs. Moxton is shielding the assassin."

"But why should she shield a murderer?"

"Ah, that you must learn from the woman herself. But if she is completely in the dark about the matter, why does she tell falsehoods? Then that cypher, those blood signs on the arm--the dying man wrote them to indicate to his wife the name of the murderer."

"You can't prove that!" cried Ellis, much excited.

"Only by deduction. Why should the man write in a cypher if his wife did not know the cypher?"

"The information, whatever it is, might have been intended for someone else."

"I don't think so. Moxton knew that his wife would be the first to discover his dead body, and wrote the message in cypher for her information. It is only reasonable to think so."

"Mrs. Moxton says she does not know what the cypher means."

"Precisely. She is telling lies and shielding the true criminal."

"How do you know that the cypher contains the name of the criminal, Harry?"

"Because I can read the cypher," was Cass's unexpected reply. "I found out the key yesterday. Look here, Bob." He jumped up from the sofa and, crossing to the writing-table, hastily scrawled two diagrams. "You see," he added, "here is a criss-cross, and a St. Andrew's cross with two letters in each angle which exhausts the alphabet."

Ellis looked at the diagrams with amazement and shook his head. "I am as much in the dark as ever. Explain."

"Well, you use the angles and the central criss-cross square for letters, with an added dot for the second letter. If you wish to write your name, 'Ellis,' in signs, you take the first letter of the third angle in the criss-cross, the two second letters of the sixth angle; the first letter of the square, and the first letter first angle St. Andrew's cross."

"I see, and 'L' being the second letter of the sixth angle you put a dot."

"Of course. If I wrote 'K' I should put no dot," replied Harry, and took a morsel of paper out of his pocket. "Here," said he, "is a copy of the sign on the dead man's arm. The second letter of ninth angle criss-cross: the first letter second angle St. Andrew's cross, and the second letter fourth angle of the same. Do you see? Now take this pencil, Bob, and use the key to turn them into letters."

Ellis did so, and produced three letters on the paper given to him. "'R U Z,'" he read slowly. "What does that mean? Is it a word?"

"I don't think so. There is no word spelt 'Ruz' in any language that I am acquainted with. I believe those three letters are the initials of the man who killed Moxton. For some reason the dying man did not desire to give up his murderer to justice, but at the same time he wished to let his wife know who struck the blow, hence the cypher. Mrs. Moxton can read the meaning, depend upon it, Bob."

"It seems strange," assented Ellis, surveying the letters thoughtfully. "Do you think there are three names here, or only two?"

"I can't say. 'R U' may mean Rupert or Rudolph, but I am in the dark so far. I have discovered the letters, Bob; it is for Mrs. Moxton to explain them to you."

"What about this other sign?" said the doctor, evading a reply.

"Well, at first I thought it was a serpent, but as it has four feet and a wriggle of a tail, I conclude it is a lizard. Mere guessing, you understand."

"What connection can it have with the letters?"

"I don't know. Ask me something easier, or rather," said Cass, with a peculiar smile, "ask Mrs. Moxton. She knows the truth about letters, and lizard and murder. But she won't tell it to you."

"Why not?" asked Ellis, angrily.

"Because, my poor fellow, I firmly believe that the murderer of Mr. Moxton is the lover of Mrs. Moxton."

CHAPTER V
MRS MOXTON SEEKS COUNSEL

Needless to say, Ellis, in his then state of mind, declined to believe that the widow had intrigued with a lover, or had--according to the theory of Cass--armed his hand with the knife. In her evidence she declared that she knew no one in Dukesfield and went nowhere, and this statement was substantiated by Mrs. Basket. The landlady, with feminine curiosity about matters which did not concern her, was as good as a detective, and from the first coming of the mysterious Moxtons to Myrtle Villa, she had watched their movements. Knowing this, Ellis made a few inquiries when Mrs. Basket was clearing the breakfast-table. Harry having already departed to Fleet Street, the doctor was alone, and conducted the examination as he pleased and at his leisure. Mrs. Basket, only too willing to talk, chattered like a parrot, and, indeed, her green dress with yellow trimmings resembled the plumage of that bird in no small degree. She was a gaudy, irresponsible gabbler.

"Bless your 'eart, sir, she didn't know no one," declared Mrs. Basket. "A prisoner in a gaol, that is what she was at Myrtle Viller; not but what she oughtn't to be in a real one. I don't say as that Moxton," Mrs. Basket shivered, "wasn't a brute in his treatment of her, but she did for him as sure as I'm a living woman. She did for him."

"The jury did not think so, Mrs. Basket!"

Mrs. Basket snorted. "A jury of them swindling tradesmen," said she, contemptuously. "What do they know of it? Mrs. Moxton killed him with the carving-knife, and threw it away arterwards.

"How do you know she threw it away?"

"'Cos it ain't in the 'ouse. Yes! you may look, an' look, doctor, but it ain't in the 'ouse. I've bin there and know."

"You have been in Myrtle Villa?" said Ellis, astonished. "Do you know Mrs. Moxton, then?"

"For the sake of law and order and Queen's justice I made it my business to know her, sir. The other morning I went over to offer to buy some of her furniture, 'earing as she was leaving Dukesfield."

Ellis jumped up. "She is not leaving Dukesfield," he denied.

"Oh, that was my idear of getting into the 'ouse," explained Mrs. Basket, complacently. "She said she wasn't, and told me so in the kitching, where it was I wished to be. Then she looked so poorly that I offered to make 'er a cup of tea, and she said I might, asking me questions about the people 'ere in the meantime."

"What sort of questions?"

"Oh, what was thought of her, and if they called her names," returned Mrs. Basket, incoherently. "But I made 'er the tea and she 'ad it. For a few minutes she went into the front parlour, and I looked in all the dresser drawers for the knife, but it wasn't there. No, doctor," repeated Mrs. Basket, with emphasis, "I do assure you it wasn't in the 'ole of that there kitching, though I searched most perticler."

"Someone might have stolen the knife."

"There weren't nobody in the 'ouse to steal it. Not a soul ever went near the viller but tradesmen, and they never got no further than the back door. Sir, I do believe as she murdered him with the knife, and 'id it way arterwards--p'r'aps in them brickfields," concluded Mrs. Basket, vaguely.

"Well, we can't be sure of that. You are certain that Mrs. Moxton had no visitors?"

"Quite, sir."

"And she saw no one?"

"Not a blessed soul save 'er 'usband as she did for. And if you'll excuse me, doctor, I've my work to look arter," whereupon the gossip waddled away with the breakfast tray.

It may appear strange that a cultured man like Ellis should listen to the coarse babblings of an uneducated woman, but he had a reason for doing so. For the sake of protecting Mrs. Moxton it was needful that he should know the gossip of the neighbourhood, and none could so well enlighten him on this point as Mrs. Basket. Several times her openly-expressed conviction of Mrs. Moxton's guilt made Ellis wince, and but for the above reason he would have ordered her out of the room. However, his self-control gained him two pieces of information; firstly, that Mrs. Moxton had received no masculine visitor since her arrival in Dukesfield, and, secondly, that the carving-knife with which the murder--from the nature of the wound--might have been committed, had disappeared. Ellis was now satisfied that the widow had no lover, but he was disturbed over the concealment or loss--he did not know which to call it--of the carving-knife. If no one but Mrs. Moxton was, or had been, in the house, she must know the whereabouts of the knife. For enlightenment on this point, and in order to satisfy his doubts, Ellis made up his mind to call on the widow, and, acting on the impulse of the moment, did so.

Strangely enough Mrs. Moxton not only welcomed him eagerly, but informed him that his arrival was opportune. "If you had not come I should have sent for you," said she, and conducted him into a cheerful little sitting-room all white paint, Chinese matting, and furniture covered with bright-hued chintz.

"What is the matter, Mrs. Moxton? There is nothing wrong, I hope."

"Oh, no! but I want your advice. You are my only friend."

"I am proud of the position, Mrs. Moxton, and I hope you will permit me, as a friend, to ask you a few plain questions?"

The little woman's resolute face grew pale. "About the death?" she murmured.

"Yes! You know that there is a slur on your name in connection with that. As your friend, I wish to remove that slur by assisting you to hunt down the murderer."

It was an odd but true thing that Mrs. Moxton had the same habit as Ellis of walking up and down the room when annoyed. At the conclusion of the doctor's last speech she rose suddenly and took a turn to compose her mind. "It is very good of you to think of helping me," she said abruptly, "but why should you?"

"Because I wish to be your friend, and I know that you are in danger."

"I am in no danger if you allude to this preposterous accusation that I killed my husband. If needs be I can protect myself should the occasion arise."

"By denouncing someone else?"

Mrs. Moxton turned on Ellis with a frown. "What do you mean?"

"Rumour says that if you did not murder Moxton yourself you know who did, and that you are shielding him."

"Him! Oh, I am shielding a man," said the widow, catching at the final word. "Set your mind at rest, doctor, I am shielding no man."

"Mrs. Moxton, why not be candid and tell me all?"

"I told all I knew at the inquest," she replied sullenly.

"Can you swear that you do not know who killed your husband?"

"I was on my oath at the inquest, I tell you," cried the woman, passionately. "I will not swear again--to you."

"Very good," said Ellis, coldly. "I see that you doubt me."

"I doubt you! I trust you more than you think. Doctor Ellis, in spite of what I said to you before, I am surrounded on all sides by difficulties and dangers. One false step and Heaven knows what may happen! I can't tell you all--I dare not. But you are my friend and must help me."

"How can I when you won't confess the truth?"

"If I only dare!" Mrs. Moxton took another turn up the room, and came back to Ellis with a more determined expression on her face. "Listen, doctor! I will tell you what I can. Afterwards you can ask me what questions you will, and I shall reply to the best of my ability. Thus we shall understand one another."

Ellis looked at her trim little figure in the black dress, at the widow's cap on the fair hair, at the candid face beneath it. As has been before stated, Mrs. Moxton was comely rather than pretty, but she had a firmly-moulded chin, a resolute expression on her lips and in her grey eyes, and was, on the whole, a woman of courage and resource. How one so sensible could have tied herself to a brute like Moxton, and could have submitted to neglect and cruelty for long months was more than Ellis could understand. Perhaps it was one of those unanswerable problems of the feminine nature which women themselves cannot explain. Ellis was puzzled, and in the hope of gaining some insight into this apparently contradictory nature, waited eagerly for the promised explanation.

"On the day after the murder--in the morning, that is," said Mrs. Moxton, "I had a visitor. His card, with the name Richard Busham, was brought to me by a charwoman I engaged, but owing to the events of the previous night I refused to see him. He went away saying he would call again, but up to the present he has not done so."

"Who is Richard Busham? Do you know him?"

"Not personally. I never saw him, and he has never met me. But he is the cousin of my late husband, the nephew of Moxton of Bond Street. Now, I believe that he came to see me about the will, and I am vexed at not having admitted him."

"Why not call on him? Have you his address?"

"I heard it from Edgar. Mr. Busham is a solicitor, and has his office in Esher Lane, near the Temple. The late Mr. Moxton, of Bond Street, was a mean, shabby man who employed the cheapest labour he could get, and I believe his nephew did all his legal business for him. Now, Edgar and Mr. Busham hated one another, and when my husband was disinherited Mr. Busham was declared heir by old Moxton. If that will held good he would not waste time coming to see me, but from the very fact of his visit I believe that Edgar's father repented at the last moment, and made a new will, leaving the property to us."

"You can make certain of that by seeing Busham."

Mrs. Moxton looked troubled. "I am afraid," she said faintly. "I am terribly afraid."

"I do not see why you should be."

"Mr. Busham called on the morning after the murder; he must have learnt then of my loss. Yet he has never repeated his visit, has never written a line. I can't conceive his reason for acting in this way, unless," here she hesitated, "he believes that I murdered Edgar."

"He would not be so foolish as to believe that without evidence, and even if he did, the inquest must have disabused his mind of the idea."

"For all that I am afraid to call. I have heard Edgar talk of Mr. Busham; he is a dangerous man, Dr. Ellis, and for all I know may be laying a trap for me."

"Tell me the truth and I will prevent your falling into this trap."

Mrs. Moxton hesitated, and then burst out defiantly: "What is it you wish to know?"

"Firstly, if you know the meaning of the blood signs on your husband's arm?"

"No! I do not."

"Then I am wiser than you, for I do."

"You!" Mrs. Moxton bit her lip. "What do you know?"

"That the signs stand for the letters R. U. Z. What the lizard, as I think it is, means I don't know. Mrs. Moxton, what is the meaning of the three letters R. U. Z.?"

"I don't know, really I don't!"

"Had your husband any friend with a name beginning Ruz, or with initials R. U. Z.?"

"Not that I ever heard of."

"What about the lizard?"

"I cannot understand its meaning."

"And you don't comprehend either the letters or the cypher?"

"No! no! no!"

This triple denial was so emphatic that Ellis was forced to believe her. Yet it appeared strange that she should be so ignorant of matters which virtually concerned the death of her husband. He looked keenly at her for some sign of confusion, but the brow of Mrs. Moxton was as open as the day. If she lied she was a wonderful actress, but Ellis did not believe that she lied, being too much in love to consider her so deliberately base.

"Well!" said he, making an attempt in another direction to fathom the mystery. "My landlady, Mrs. Basket, called to see you the other day."

"To spy out the land. Oh, I saw through her pretended kindness at once. She wished to find some proof of my guilt, but as I had nothing to conceal I gave her the opportunity of convincing herself that I was innocent."

"The very proof you gave convinced her of your guilt," said Ellis, warmly. "Mrs. Basket is a dangerous woman, Mrs. Moxton; one of those well-meaning people who do so much harm. She has no special grudge against you, but she has got it into her mind that you killed your husband with the carving-knife."

"But I did not. It is nonsense talking like that!"

"Then where is the carving-knife? Mrs. Basket searched but could not find it, and now she believes that you have hidden it."

"What rubbish!" said Mrs. Moxton, with contempt. "Edgar threw it away."

"Threw it away? Why?"

"Because he knew that I kept it by me to protect myself against tramps or burglars, so, out of sheer devilry, the week before he died, he threw it into the garden behind some bushes."

"Is it there now?"

"No. I searched everywhere for it after the murder and could not find it. Why do you ask?"

"Because a broad-bladed knife was used to kill your husband, and it might have been the carving-knife. The murderer must have picked it up and made use of it. And----"

The woman appeared uneasy, and interrupted Ellis. "How would the murderer know that the knife was in the garden? Only two people knew where it was thrown. One was Edgar, the other myself."

"I would not advise you to say that in public, Mrs. Moxton, as people might count it as good circumstantial evidence that you killed Moxton."

"Oh!" cried the widow, clenching her fists. "Do you believe me guilty?"

"No, I do not. Is there any need to ask me that question?"

"Why? why? You have plenty of evidence against me. I have placed myself in your hands by confessing about the carving-knife. Why do you not denounce me as guilty?"

"How can you ask?" cried Ellis, carried out of his usual equable self by her vehemence. "Don't you know--can't you see--I love you! I love you! that is why I believe you guiltless."

CHAPTER VI
A FRESH DISCOVERY

In placing herself in the dock, so to speak, Mrs. Moxton had been defiant, loud-voiced and reckless, daring Ellis to denounce her for a crime of which she knew herself innocent. His refusal, and the cause he gave for such refusal, took her by surprise. Long since she had guessed that the doctor loved her, but she did not count on his proclaiming the fact so soon. Nor would he have done so had he not been thrown off his guard by her appeal. But her demand and his answer to it produced on both sides a stupefied calm. Ellis, frightened at his own boldness, remained silent after uttering the fatal words; Mrs. Moxton, on the other hand, felt her wrath die away in sheer surprise. Then her cheeks flushed from an unexplained emotion, and a light beamed from her eyes.

"You love me!" she murmured softly, and looked at Ellis.

Something in her regard, her tone, in her whole attitude, seemed to melt the frozen silence of the man. He sprang forward and touched her hand.

"You are not angry?" he asked, with eagerness.

The touch recalled Mrs. Moxton to a sense of what she owed to herself, and woke in her a feeling of wrath at the audacity of the man, who could speak the word to a woman lately widowed in so terrible a manner.

"How dare you!" she cried angrily, retreating. "What must you think of me to talk like that!"

"I think the world of you," replied Ellis, doggedly. "I have said the truth."

"You deceive yourself. What you take for the truth is fantasy. You cannot love one whom you have known only three weeks."

"Love can be born of a glance."

"In romances, I grant, but not in real life." She paused and burst out laughing. "Oh, it is too absurd."

Ellis was piqued. "I fail to see the absurdity. I speak as I feel."

For the moment Mrs. Moxton appeared to meditate an answer to this plain statement. Suddenly she bit her lip, drew back and shook her head. "You speak folly. You think madness," she said. "Consider! I am a three weeks' widow. My husband died by violence, and his death is not avenged. My name is smirched. My--no! This is no time for such talk. Let us forget the words you have uttered."

"I cannot forget."

"Then I must lose my friend," said Mrs. Moxton, determinedly. "I really cannot meet you on these terms. I am a newly-made widow, not a possible wife for you."

"But in the future?"

"Let the future look after itself," she cried petulantly. "What we have to do, is to attend to the present. You wish to help me. Do so by leaving this crime to be punished by Heaven."

"But your smirched name?"

"I can bear that. I have borne worse things. Oh, do not look so astonished, Dr. Ellis. I have had a queer up-and-down, topsy-turvy sort of life. Some day I may tell it to you, but we don't know each other well enough for that yet. If I find that you deserve my confidence---" She broke off the sentence abruptly. "Never mind that now. I have work to do. Yes! I shall take your advice about calling on Mr. Busham. This very day I shall call and ask him about the will. Could you meet me here at three o'clock, doctor?"

Ellis felt his breath taken away by the boldness of the demand. "If you wish me to come."

"Of course I wish it or I would not ask. Remember, doctor, you are my friend. No, don't repeat that folly. We are comrades at present, nothing more. You do not understand me now. You will when I explain."

"Will you ever explain?"

"Yes! No! I can't say. So much depends upon what kind of a man I find you to be. Now, go, please, as I must dress for my visit. Mind, I shall expect you at three o'clock, to tell you the result of my interview."

"At three o'clock," repeated Ellis, earnestly, and so they parted.

When the doctor found himself in the broad, cheerful sunshine of the Jubilee Road he was not quite certain if he was asleep or awake. To him Mrs. Moxton was more of an enigma than the murder itself. He could not understand her attitude, nor could he guess what motive she had in acting thus strangely. She was apparently pleased that he loved her; she was angry at his abrupt declaration; he could not gain her confidence; yet she requested him to meet her at three o'clock to ask his advice about her visit. What was he to understand from such a medley of contradictions? He sought in his own mind for every possible explanation, but could find none, so concluding that it was the more sensible course to possess his soul in patience until this sphinx explained her own riddle, he returned home. Here, to his surprise, he found a friend of the morbid lady's come to consult him about her heart, and in the joy of such promise of an increasing practice he forgot Mrs. Moxton and her eccentricities. In a similar situation a woman would not have forgotten, but Byron's lines give the reason for that:

"Man's love is of man's life a thing apart;
'Tis woman's whole existence."

Nevertheless, when his mind was less occupied with material things, the feeling about Mrs. Moxton revived, and he waited impatiently for the hour of three. It would seem that circumstances were about to involve him in the drama,--it might be tragedy--of this woman's life, and he felt eager for the call to step on the stage. What part would be assigned to him he could not guess. Was he to be the husband of the heroine or merely the friend, or would he pose as the foil to that shadowy lover in whose existence and guilt Cass believed? Altogether Ellis was in the dark, afraid to venture forward for fear of the unknown. He waited for a hand to draw him on to his doom--in plain English, for the hand and guidance of Mrs. Moxton. These strange thoughts, passing through the doctor's mind, made him fear that its usually accurate balance was disturbed.

Shortly after three o'clock struck from the bran-new brick tower of the bran-new Dukesfield church, he saw her walking briskly down the road. Even in his pre-occupation he noted her trim figure, the decided way in which she set down and lifted her feet, and the general air of alert resolution which stamped her whole being. Here was a woman of mind, of decision, of character, with few feminine failings, and more than ever Ellis wondered at her past history, as related by herself at the inquest. He began to suspect that there might be something after all in the ideas of Harry Cass. Mrs. Basket declared the woman "was a deep 'un." That also might be true.

"Good news! good news!" cried Mrs. Moxton, when she arrived. "I have seen Mr. Busham and I am right. Old Moxton made a will leaving the property to Edgar."

"But he is dead. How do you stand now?"

The widow let the gate click behind her, and walked up the path with a wrinkled brow, betokening thought. "That depends upon Edgar's will."

"Did he make one?"

"I think so. In one of his good humours he made a will leaving all his property to me. I believe the will was signed and witnessed at Monte Carlo. He told me about it, but I never saw it."

"Then how do you know it exists?"

"Edgar told me of it," repeated Mrs. Moxton. "It will no doubt be in his despatch-box, or in this room."

By this time the pair were again in the cheerful parlour, and her gaze was fixed upon a well-filled bookcase. "I should not wonder if it was hidden amongst the books," said Mrs. Moxton, pensively.

Ellis showed some amazement at this strange remark. "Why should he have put a valuable document amongst his books, Mrs. Moxton?"

The widow sat down and signed to Ellis to do likewise. "My dear doctor, do you know anything about drunken men?"

This was even a stranger remark than the former.

"I have come into contact with them," said Ellis, with a slight smile, "but what has that to do with this will?"

"More than you think," she retorted. "Edgar was never very sane at the best of times; but when drunk, as he often was, he took leave of his senses completely. Drunken men, as I daresay you know, have each their various idiosyncrasies which display the true animal within. Edgar's indwelling animal was a magpie."

"Oh!" The doctor seized on her meaning at once. "You believe that he concealed things!"

"Yes! When drunk he would hide his watch, chain, jewellery, money, and when sober could not remember where he put them. I was set to hunt them out, and often found them in that bookcase. Lately he took to hiding papers, so it is not unlikely he concealed his will. However, it may be in his despatch-box after all. That is in the bedroom, and I have the keys, so I shall go and look. In the meantime, doctor, would you turn out those books and see if it is concealed there?"

"Certainly; but one moment, Mrs. Moxton," he added as she was about to leave the room; "if your husband has left no will, what becomes of the property?"

"Half goes to Mr. Busham as the next-of-kin, and half to me as the widow, but, of course, I get all if Edgar left a will in my favour."

"Mr. Busham won't like that."

"No!" Mrs. Moxton frowned. "I'll tell you what he is," she burst out; "a mean, grasping miser. His manner to me was most disagreeable. I feel sure he suspects me of the murder. While he can get half the property I daresay he will hold his tongue, but if all comes to me I am certain he will make trouble."

"About the murder?"

"Yes, but I am not afraid. I can defend myself, and I have you for a friend."

"But what can I do?"

"Defend me!" Mrs. Moxton threw a searching glance at the amazed face of Ellis. "Look for the will," she said abruptly, and left the room.

By this time the doctor's capacity for astonishment was completely exhausted. Mrs. Moxton's conduct became more extraordinary at every interview, and it was worse than useless trying to account for it. Only further acquaintance and observation could explain her personality and apparently purposeless remarks; therefore Ellis, taking this sensible view, devoted himself to the task of searching for the will.

The bookcase was of white-painted wood, of no great size, and with three shelves. French novels in yellow and green paper covers predominated and Ellis tumbled these ruthlessly on to the floor. To all appearance the taste of the late Mr. Moxton had not been over-refined, for the majority of the novels were by the most sensual Parisian authors. But mingled with these decadent works were a number of old-fashioned books, mostly educational, with here and there a slim old-fashioned volume of travels. For the first ten minutes of his search Ellis paid no attention to these, but looked for the will at the back of the shelves. It was not to be found in any one of them, but he came across an amazing number of music-hall programmes, headed: "The Merryman, Viper Street, Soho." Evidently someone had been an assiduous attendant at this place of amusement, if the programmes were to be taken as evidence.

"Moxton!" said Ellis to himself, when this idea occurred to him. "So this is where he went night after night." He examined the dates of the programmes. "Yes! all within the last three months, one night after another. H'm! Mrs. Moxton said that she did not know where her husband went, yet these programmes must have informed her even if he held his tongue. Extraordinary woman! I can't understand her actions or denials."

Failing to find the will on the shelves, Ellis examined the books. One of these, a fat little brown volume, entitled, *The Universal Informer*, was inscribed on the flyleaf, "Janet Gordon, from her father, Thomas Gordon, Edinburgh," both of which names were unknown to Ellis. The book opened of itself at a turned-down page, on which was set forth a list of the towns and cities of the world. Now, what struck Ellis as strange was the fact that the turned-down page was towards the end of the list, and contained the towns beginning with "Z." This was one of the letters concealed in the blood signs, and to say the least it is not a letter generally used. Wondering if he was on the track of a discovery, Ellis glanced down the page. His eye caught the word "lizard," and he eagerly read the paragraph in which it was contained. Four lines informed him that "Zirknitz is a town in Austria, and that in its environs is found a peculiar species of lizard." Ellis reflected. "On the arm was the letter 'Z' concealed in a sign, and the representation of a lizard. This book, which opens of itself at this particular page, mentions an Austrian town called Zirknitz and a peculiar lizard. There must be some connection between the murder and this paragraph, but I can't see it myself. What can an Austrian town have to do with the crime in Jubilee Road?"

Finding no answer to this question he pursued his search. The old-fashioned books seemed to belong to Thomas Gordon, of Edinburgh, but in one or two he had inscribed their presentation to his "daughter Janet," or to his "daughter Laura."

"Laura!" murmured Ellis. "That is Mrs. Moxton's name. Perhaps she is the Laura Gordon who owns these books. In fact, she must be. If so, she has a sister Janet; it is the first I have heard of her sister. Hullo, what's this?"

"This" was a novel of Catulle Mendes, which had a name scribbled in pencil on the outside. The name was "Rudolph Zirknitz."

"R. U. Z.," said the doctor, staring at the pencilled autograph; "so it stands for Rudolph Zirknitz, who evidently takes his name and the totem of the lizard from that Austrian town."

At this moment Mrs. Moxton entered with a disconsolate air. "Have you found the will, doctor?" she inquired; "it is not in the despatch-box."

"No, Mrs. Moxton, I have not found the will, but I have learnt the name of the man who killed your husband."

The widow became as grey as the wall-paper, and leant against the door for support. "What? Who? I--I do not understand," she gasped.

"The murderer is called Rudolph Zirknitz," explained Ellis. "Now, who is Rudolph Zirknitz?"

Mrs. Moxton made no attempt to answer this question. Closing her eyes she slipped quietly on to the floor, and lay at the feet of Ellis, white and insensible.

CHAPTER VII
WHAT THE CABMAN KNEW

When Cass returned from his day's work he found Ellis impatiently expecting him. The doctor looked ill and worried. On hearing his friend's footstep he rushed into the passage and half-led, half-dragged him into the room. Harry was much surprised at this unusual excitement on the part of Ellis.

"What the deuce is the matter, Bob? You are as pale as a muffin, and your hair is all over the--"

"Harry! Harry! Never mind my looks. I am nearly worried out of my life by this--this murder."

"Or by Mrs. Moxton--have you made any discoveries?"

"Yes. I have discovered the meaning of the letters R. U. Z., and of the lizard sign."

"By Jove!" Cass in his turn became excited. "Well, well, go on--go on."

"The letters are the initials of a man's name."

"The murderer's name?"

"I don't say that, and yet he might be the criminal. I said so to--"

"But the name, Bob, the name?"

"Rudolph Zirknitz."

"H'm! A foreigner?"

"An Austrian. He takes his name from a town called Zirknitz, in Austria, which has in its environs a peculiar sort of lizard found nowhere else."

"Ho! ho! Now comes in the 'totem' of our assassin. How did you find this out?"

The doctor sat down and rapidly detailed his discoveries, and how they were brought about by the search for the will. "I revived Mrs. Moxton from her faint," he concluded, "but she refused to answer a single question. In the end I was forced to leave her, and for the last few hours I have been in a state of distraction. I am so glad you are back. Put your sharp wits to work, Harry, and tell me what it all means."

"I told you before," replied Cass, coolly, "and you flew in a rage with me, saying that I had no grounds for the statement. Now you have learned the grounds, and I repeat my belief. This Zirknitz is the lover of Mrs. Moxton, and she is shielding him from the consequences of having killed her husband--no doubt at her request."

"I can't--I won't believe it of that poor woman, Harry."

"Facts are stubborn things, Bob. The case is as clear as noonday to me."

Ellis, still believing in the innocence of the woman he loved, would have replied somewhat violently to this declaration, but that Mrs. Basket entered with the supper. It was now seven o'clock, for since Cass had been appointed critic to the *Early Bird* they had altered the meal from nine to seven. In a few minutes Mrs. Basket, not being encouraged to chatter on this particular night, left the room wondering what could be the matter with her gentlemen. Ellis trifled with his food, feeling too worried to enjoy it, but the less nervous Cass did full justice to Mrs. Basket's idea of an Irish stew. Between mouthfuls he talked and answered the doctor's objections.

"It is all nonsense Mrs. Basket saying that Mrs. Moxton had no visitors. Both she and her husband, from what you tell me, must be shady people. Poor devil! He is dead, so let us say no ill of him. But Mrs. Moxton. I daresay she received visitors at night when Mrs. Basket and her tradesmen spies were not about."

"You have no grounds for making such an accusation," fumed Ellis.

"Keep calm, Bob. I am speaking without prejudice. No grounds! Well, if I have not, why did Mrs. Moxton faint at the mention of that name? Why did she lie about the signs? Why did she feign ignorance of the place where her husband went every night? She must have known. I tell you, Bob, that Mrs. Moxton is fighting every inch, and I daresay she is angry at your persistence in following up the case. Come, now, own up! Did she not ask you to leave the matter alone?"

"Well, she did," admitted the doctor, with reluctance. "I confess that I do not understand Mrs. Moxton. Her acts are doubtful, her words are strange, and I agree with you that she knows more about this matter than she chooses to confess. All the same, Harry, I am not an absolute fool, even where women are concerned; and there is something in Mrs. Moxton's looks and manner which satisfies me that she is a true, good, pure, brave woman."

"H'm! her conduct does not justify the use of a single adjective of that sort."

"I know! I know! All the same, I believe in her."

"Because you are in love, and love is blind."

"Rubbish! I don't believe in that worn-out saying. I can see Mrs. Moxton's imperfections as plainly as you can. She is not a saint by any manner of means,--but a sinner? No, Harry, I cannot believe she is what you make her out. If she inspired the murder, why does she not run away?"

"Because she is fighting for her fortune, old boy."

"But she is not even certain that a will is in existence."

"So she says," replied Cass, pouring himself out some beer; "but I beg leave to doubt that artless pose. It is my firm conviction that she knew of old Moxton's repentance and eleventh-hour testament, that she got her husband to make his will in her favour, and that she induced her lover, Zirknitz, to put him out of the way so that they might enjoy the money together. It is to reap the fruits of the crime that she stays on here, Bob."

"That is all theory."

"So was my earlier statement, yet it has been proved true by yourself. I daresay M. Zirknitz came to see Mrs. Moxton in the evening when her husband was at the Merryman Music-Hall."

"I never heard of that place, Harry."

"Perhaps not. It has been in existence only for two years. The usual variety entertainment, you know. A man called Otto Schwartz keeps it."

"A German?"

"A typical lager-beer German. Not at all a bad fellow, either."

Dr. Ellis slowly lighted his pipe. "I wonder why Moxton went so regularly to that place?" he said reflectively.

"Well, he might have gone there to make love to one of the ladies who do the turns, but I rather think," said Cass, significantly, "that his object was to gamble. From all his wife says about Monte Carlo and other places the man was a confirmed card-sharper."

"But gambling is not allowed in London."

"No doubt. A good many vices are not allowed in this most immaculate of cities, in this Tartuffe of capitals, but they exist all the same. I don't know for certain, nobody does, but it is rumoured that there is a secret gambling-hell connected with the apparently innocent music-hall of Herr Schwartz's."

Ellis glanced at his watch. "It is getting on for eight o'clock," he remarked. "Let us go to Soho to-night."

"If you like. I have no particular engagement. But your reason?"

"I want to learn all I can about Moxton. If he went there to gamble, Herr Schwartz will know of him. Also we might learn something of Zirknitz. As the book proves, the autograph also, he was a friend of Moxton's, so it is not unlikely he went with him to this secret hell you talk of."

"Very good; let us go at once," said Cass, rising. "But as you and I seem to have become amateur detectives, let us conduct our case with due discretion. There is one piece of evidence we have overlooked."

"What is that?"

"The cab-stand."

"The cab-stand! And what has that to do with the murder?"

"Bob! Bob! You can write about eyes and their diseases, but you cannot make use of your own optics. It is probable that the murderer of Moxton, this Zirknitz, wished to get away as speedily as possible from the scene of his crime, so it is equally probable that he made for the cab-stand."

"Or the railway station."

"That is much further away. The cab-stand is comparatively near the Jubilee Road."

"But no cabman came forward at the inquest."

"I daresay. No cabman had any right to suspect his fare of murder. But we will question those on the rank before we go to Soho. Let us find out if Mr. Zirknitz took a cab between a quarter-past and half-past eleven."

Ellis shrugged his shoulders. "As you please. But it seems to me futile to waste time in asking questions which cannot be answered."

"We have yet to learn if our time is being wasted," retorted Cass, and ending the conversation for the time being, the young men left the house.

By this time Cass had become quite eager to solve the mystery, and willingly placed his quick wit and indomitable perseverance at the service of his friend. He admired Ellis greatly, and there was quite a David and Jonathan feeling between the two. It annoyed Cass to think that the doctor might throw away his life on such a woman as he believed Mrs. Moxton to be; and he undertook the case in the hope of proving her unworthiness. At the present moment appearances were decidedly against her, yet in the face of such black evidence Ellis still clung to his belief in her. This instinctive feeling, based on no reasonable foundation, was so insisted upon by Ellis that his friend became quite angry.

"It is the most sensible men who become the greatest fools on occasions," he said, with the rough speech of intimate friendship. "You have known this woman only three weeks, and you are absolutely ignorant of her past life save what she has chosen to tell you. The circumstantial and actual evidence points to her not only as a shady person, but as a positive criminal, yet in the face of it all you look upon her as a saint."

"No, I don't. I told you so before; but I feel sure she is a good woman. I can give you no reason, but I myself am satisfied without one. As to your evidence, Harry, you know the most innocent person can be wrongly accused, can be even hanged on evidence which, false as it is, appears sufficient. There is the Lesurques case, for--"

"Oh! the Courier of Lyons. I know. And I can quote you at least a dozen others. All the same, I don't believe in Mrs. Moxton."

"Well, I do. For all you know she may be protecting her sister."

Cass stopped short. "Has she a sister?" he asked.

"I believe so. At least, in the books I told you about, Thomas Gordon had written the names of his daughters Laura and Janet Gordon. The first is, of course, Mrs. Moxton, the second name must be that of her sister."

"Perhaps. But the sister may be dead, may be absent from England. In any event, I do not see how you can connect her at all with the murder."

The doctor had no reply to this pertinent observation, as, after all, his remark about the sister had been made vaguely and without any ulterior meaning. A turn of the street brought them to the cab-stand at which Cass, as a journalist, was well known. He immediately began to question the men in a chaffing, popular way. They were ready enough to answer his questions, the more so as these were concerning the murder; but one and all declared that no particular man had hired a cab between eleven and twelve on the night of August 16th.

"Old Ike is the one to know, though," said a red-faced cabman. "He 'ave a memory like 'is own 'orse."

There was a murmur of assent at this, and old Ike, shaky, lean, ancient, more like a grey wolf than a man, was routed out of the shelter in which he was refreshing himself with tea.

"A fare on that murder night, sir? Lor', I don't quite know wot t' say 'bout that. 'Leven an' twelve was it? Well, now, sir, the chapsies at that time were at the station waiting the thayater trains. Weren't you, chapsies?"

"Ah! that we were, but you worn't, Ike," said the red-faced cabman, replying for the others. "You never does go fur them late fares."

"I wos alone on the rank, Mr. Cass, now I thinks of it, and I 'ad a fare to Pimlico, to Geneva Square, where that Silent 'Ouse murder took place."

"What was the man like?" asked Ellis, eagerly.

"It weren't no man, sir, but a gal, a short gal with a grey dress and a black cloak, straw 'at, fair 'air, plump figger, and small 'ands."

"Why, Cass, he is describing Mrs. Moxton," said Ellis, wonderingly. "At what time did she take your cab, Ike?"

"Just afore arf-past 'leven, sir. Came tearing down the road wild-like and crying fit to break 'er 'eart. Jus' tumbled into m'keb, she did, an' tole me to drive t' Pimlico."

"Mrs. Moxton was in our room at half-past eleven," said Cass, when finding that this was all the information obtainable they walked away. "The woman can't be Mrs. Moxton. Yet the description, fair hair, trim figure, might pass for her. I wonder who she is?"

"I know, Harry. I was right, after all. The woman who cried and fled like a guilty person was Janet Gordon, the sister of Mrs. Moxton."

CHAPTER VIII
A MUSIC-HALL STAR

It would seem, then, from this fresh discovery, that a third person was implicated in the matter, and that person a woman. Cass and Ellis argued the matter at great length in the train, and continued their argument as they drove from St. James's Station to Soho. The doctor was convinced from old Ike's description that the woman could be no other than Mrs. Moxton's sister, but Cass was more than doubtful.

"It might be a general resemblance," he said. "Besides, if Janet Gordon came to see Mrs. Moxton on that night, why does not her sister say so?"

"She is shielding her, I tell you," insisted Ellis. "That accounts for the way in which she keeps silent even to me, whom she knows as her friend."

"Why should Mrs. Moxton shield her sister, Bob? You don't suspect Janet of the crime?"

"Oh, no. From the blood-signs it is plain that Zirknitz murdered him. I don't know what to think. But it is plain that Janet was at the house that night, and perhaps she fled in terror on seeing the crime committed. However, I shall ask Mrs. Moxton about the matter."

"She will tell you nothing."

"Now that I have found out so much I think she will, if only to exonerate her sister," retorted Ellis. "If she refuses, I shall go to Geneva Square, in Pimlico, and interview Miss Gordon myself. She may have seen Zirknitz kill the poor devil, and then have fled to avoid being mixed up in the matter."

"Well," said Cass, as the cab drew up before a brilliantly-lighted portal, "it seems to me that Zirknitz is the man to catch and question. We may hear about him here, as it appears he was a companion of the dead man. But the case gets more involved at every fresh discovery. First we suspect Mrs. Moxton, then our suspicions rest on the Austrian, finally an unknown sister seems to be implicated in the matter. It will be a queer story when all things are brought to light. I hope we shall find Zirknitz here."

"If he is a wise man you will not," replied Ellis, as they alighted. "Remember, a *fac-simile* of these blood-signs appeared in all the papers. Zirknitz may know the cypher, and, having read his own initials, has, no doubt, made himself scarce."

"H'm! There is something in that. We shall see."

The music-hall was vast and palatial, with a domed roof, two galleries, and much ornate decoration. The seats were cushioned with red velvet, the promenades were carpeted. In many corners tall mirrors reflected back the moving crowd, and everywhere there was gilding, light, crystal and colour. The whole place was filled with changing hues like a king-opal, and glittered with overpowering splendour in the floods of white radiance pouring from clusters of electric lamps. A fine orchestra was playing a swinging waltz, the last movement of a ballet, and the stage was filled with a multitude of gyrating, pirouetting women, constantly moving and tossing in gorgeous costumes, like a bed of tulips in a high wind. For a few moments the two men, coming out of the dark night, were dazzled by the glare, and stunned by the crash of the music and babel of voices. Cass drew his friend aside to a marble-topped table and ordered drinks while he looked at the programme. Suddenly he caught sight of a man he knew and jumped up to shake hands.

"Hullo! Schwartz," he cried. "Here is a friend of mine I wish to introduce. Captain Garret, I hope I see you well?"

The German was a fat, fair man, quiet in looks and dress, and with a somewhat careworn face. His companion, a tall, dissipated, military gentleman, in accurate evening dress, answered to the name of Garret, and bowed distantly. This latter had a bad expression and a pair of shifty eyes.

"Ah, mine goot Cass," said Schwartz, with a beaming smile, "you haf not peen here for dis long time. And your frend?"

"Dr. Ellis," said Cass; "a well-known medical man, who has written a standard work on 'Diseases of the Eye.'"

Ellis laughed, and was about to protest against having this greatness thrust upon him, when Captain Garret turned his worn face towards him with a look of keen interest.

"Dr. Ellis," said he, in an abrupt voice, "glad to see you, very glad. Have read your book, so has Schwartz here."

"Dat is zo, mine frend. It is a goot book, and I am glad zat you gome here, doctor. Why did you not zay you gome, Cass? I would haf given tickets."

"Both of you have read my book?" said the doctor, considerably taken aback by this unexpected fame. "In Heaven's name why? It is unusual for laymen to read a treatise of that kind."

"Ah," replied Garret, with infinite sadness, "Schwartz and I are old friends, and we have good reason to read your book." He paused for a moment, then added abruptly: "My daughter is blind."

"Ach! Zat liddle Hilda She has gatterack of the eyes, poor anchel."

"My daughter has cataract of the eyes, doctor," translated Garret, "and we have tried every surgeon in Europe to cure them, but without success. Your book impressed us greatly, and now that we have met you I hope you will come and see my poor girl."

"Come and zee her effry tay, doctor. I vill pay money. If zat--" Schwartz never finished his speech. At that moment a tumult, created by some drunken man, called him away, and with a nod to Ellis he hurried off. The Captain waited only long enough to thrust his card into the doctor's hand, and also departed, while the two friends resumed their seats at the table.

"Captain W. E. Garret, Goethe Cottage, Alma Road, Parkmere," read Ellis from the card. "Why, that is the next suburb to Dukesfield."

"Oh, Schwartz lives in that quarter, does he?"

"No! not Schwartz--Garret."

"That is the same thing," replied Cass, sipping his brandy and soda; "they live together--have done so for years. Garret has the gentlemanly looks, and Schwartz the money."

"A strange pair. Who are they?"

"A couple of adventurers. Schwartz is the better of the two, though, for, from what I hear, Garret was kicked out of the army for cheating at cards. The German started this show two years ago, and took Garret to live with him; why, I don't know, unless it is that he is so fond of the daughter."

"Hilda Garret," said Ellis, recalling the name; "is she blind?"

"I believe so. Schwartz is an old bachelor, and has given all his heart to the poor girl. She is sixteen years old, I believe, and he takes care both of her and her father."

"Garret seems to be fond of his child."

"Oh, that is a pose for the benefit of Schwartz. If he didn't love Hilda the German would kick him out. Garret killed his wife with ill-treatment, and was on the fair way to exterminate Hilda when Schwartz interposed and became her good angel. Now the old scoundrel, Garret, behaves well to her, knowing that in such way he can manage Schwartz."

"You seem to know all about it, Cass!"

"I hear all the gossip, Bob. It may be true or it may not, but I am certain that Schwartz and Garret have been together these ten years carrying on their rascalities."

"Are they rascals?"

Cass laughed and nodded. "Rumour says very much so, but Schwartz is the more lovable scoundrel of the two. There is something pathetic in the way in which he clings to that blind girl."

"'There lives some soul of good in all things evil,'" quoted Ellis. "Well, I shall call at Goethe Cottage and see what I can do for the girl. If I can cure her after all the European surgeons have failed it will be a feather in my cap. Business is rolling in at last, old fellow."

"About time," said Cass, in satisfied tones. "You'll ride in your carriage yet, Bob."

The doctor laughed at this prophecy. It did not seem so impossible of realisation now as it had once been. Then he turned his attention to the stage, on which a stout lady in the shortest of skirts was favouring the audience with a song and interpolated dance of the orthodox pattern:--

"For I 'ave a little feller on the string,

(Dance)

And on me 'and he's put a little ring,

(Dance)

To the little chorch this little gal he'll taike,
She'll kiss 'im for his own sweet saike,
And he'll love 'er as 'is little bit of caike."

(Dance)

"That is Polly Horley," said Cass, referring to the singer of this gem. "She is a great favourite here."

"I don't wonder," replied Ellis, drearily; "the song is senseless enough to please even this brainless audience. Why must a music-hall ditty consist of bad English and worse grammar, delivered with a Cockney accent? Polly Horley! I know her! When I was house surgeon at St. Jude's Hospital she was brought in with a broken leg. We were excellent friends."

"Or great pals, as Miss Horley would put it. Let us send round your card and ask for an interview.'

"For what reason? I don't want to see that stout female."

"My dear fellow, Polly has been a star here since Schwartz opened the hall, and she, if anyone, will know about Moxton and Zirknitz."

"By Jove! that is true, Harry. You are a better detective than I am. Get that waiter there to take round our cards."

A small fee soon accomplished this, and the venal waiter vanished, shortly to reappear with the message that Miss Horley would be pleased to see Dr. Ellis and friend in her dressing-room after the singing of her great patriotic song. Almost immediately afterwards she marched to the footlights in the costume of Britannia, and carrying the Union Jack. Then followed the usual piece of Jingoism about "never shall be slaves, while the banner waves, earth is thick with British graves," etc., etc. The flag was duly waved at the end of each verse, and the audience, as in duty bound, joined in with imperial ardour. While Miss Horley treated the listeners to an extra verse bearing on the local situation, Ellis and Harry Cass were guided into the back regions of the stage by a smart page-boy. He led them through a wilderness of scenes, along dark passages, and past rooms thronged with ballet girls, ultimately ushering them into a small apartment, barely furnished and flooded with unshaded electric light. Here the visitors were accommodated with two chairs, and shortly Britannia, flag and all, made her noisy appearance. She literally threw herself on the doctor.

"I'm that glad to see you again, doc," cried Britannia, effusively. "Where have you been hiding all this time?" Then, without waiting for an answer, she turned to Harry: "You're a stranger, too, Mr. Cass, but better late than never. I am glad to see you. You'll both have drinks, I s'pose?"

"No, thank you, Miss Horley. We just wish to congratulate you on your new song."

"Ah, it knocks 'em, don't it?" said the fair Polly. "They never let me off without a triple encore. You are looking ill, doctor. It's that 'orrid murder, eh?"

"What murder?"

"Why, the Dukesfield murder, silly! I saw all about it in the papers; your name was there, too, and I said: 'Here's my dear old pal Ellis, who mended my spar.'"

"Oh, you said that, did you?"

"Rather. It was queer that you should be the doctor to see after that poor chap. I call him poor chap because he is dead," explained Miss Horley, "but I never did like that Moxton. A miserly, insulting crab-stick."

"Oh, so you knew Moxton?"

"Of course I did. He came here nearly every night. What is more, he took his wife from here."

Ellis was painfully excited. "Mrs. Moxton? Was she a music-hall singer?"

"Not she," replied Polly, disdainfully. "She hadn't the brains to sing. She typed for a living, I believe, but her sister was a programme-seller here."

"Janet Gordon?"

"Oh, you know her, Mr. Cass, do you?"

"No, I don't, but I have heard of her."

"Then I'll bet you heard nothing but good of her," cried Miss Horley, warmly. "That girl is as square a woman as ever lived. If it hadn't been for her, goodness knows what would have become of that silly little Laura."

"I don't call Mrs. Moxton silly," said the doctor, annoyed by this description.

"Oh, don't you, doctor, then I do. She was silly to marry that beast of a Moxton, the horrid little cad. It was against Janet's wish that she did so, and Janet was right. A nice mess she made of her life. He neglected her, and came here to make love to me--me, a married woman with five of a family. But I slapped his face for him," said Polly, complacently, "that I did."

"Mrs. Moxton met her husband here?"

"Yes. Janet let her come to the hall sometimes, and she met Moxton. Both girls are decent, doc, so don't say that I run 'em down. Janet is a girl in a thousand. She left us a week or two ago. I expect she has gone to live with her sister now. They will have old Moxton's money, I daresay."

"Who do you think killed Moxton?" asked Cass.

"My dear boy, ask me something easier," said Polly, applying the powder-puff to her nose. "I haven't the slightest idea. He was nasty enough to have any quantity of enemies."

"Do you know a man called Zirknitz, Miss Horley?"

Polly turned round with a smile. "Do I know the nose on my face?" she said lightly. "Of course I do. It is funny you should talk of him, for he is coming to see me in a few minutes. If you'll wait, I'll introduce him to you."

Ellis and Cass exchanged looks of congratulation at this good fortune, and the unsuspicious Polly, little thinking she was weaving a halter for a man's neck, babbled on. "He might have found out the truth if he'd only gone to Dukesfield on that night as he intended."

"Did he go there?" asked Ellis, eagerly.

"No. Janet was there on that night. She got leave from Schwartz to see her sister. Zirknitz, who is a friend of Janet's, intended calling for her to take her home, but Moxton got drunk here, and Zirknitz didn't go lest there should be a row. So--come in." She broke off as there was a sharp knock.

The door opened, and a handsome, light-haired young man appeared.

"Oh! here you are," cried Polly, jovially. "Doc, this is Mr. Rudolph Zirknitz."

CHAPTER IX
THE AUSTRIAN

Cass and Ellis examined the new-comer swiftly as they returned his bow. It was a foreign bow, including a smart click of the heels. Zirknitz was tall, slim, and remarkably handsome, his good looks being set off to the fullest advantage by the quiet perfection of his evening dress. He wore no jewellery, the whitest of linen, the neatest of bows, and a silk hat with a wonderful lustre. As the night was chilly he had on a fur-lined coat with sable cuffs and collar, and his slender hands, encased in grey gloves, held a gold-topped bamboo. Altogether Mr., or Monsieur, or Herr Zirknitz was, to all appearances, a man who valued his looks as part of his stock-in-trade to enable him to carry on his business of adventurer. But, in spite of his care, the hoof betrayed the devil, for there was a rakish, fast air about him which stamped him as dangerous. Ellis thought that such a scamp would not draw the line at murder, so long as he could save himself from punishment.

"I am charmed to meet your friends, madame," said Zirknitz, in good enough English, but with a pronounced foreign accent. "And the names?"

"This is Mr. Cass; that gent is Dr. Ellis."

The smile died away on the Austrian's lips. "Ellis!" he said, in a hesitating manner, "and a doctor--of Dukesfield?"

"Yes, M. Zirknitz," replied Ellis, grimly, "of Dukesfield."

"You saw the body of my poor friend Moxton?"

"Yes. Were you a friend of his?"

"The best friend he had, monsieur. If I knew who killed him so cruelly, I would spend my life trying to bring him to justice. *Helas!*"

"H'm!" repeated Cass. "So you think a man killed Moxton?"

"I go by the evidence at the inquest," said Zirknitz, with a bow. "The doctor explained at the inquest that a man must have struck the blow."

"I said that indeed, M. Zirknitz. But a woman may be mixed up in the matter."

"Here, all of you!" cried Polly, with impatient good humour, "I can't have you three talking here all night. I want to dress and go home to my chicks. Rudolph, you must come and see me on another night. Mr. Cass, doctor, look up yours truly whenever you get a chance, and good-night to you, my dears."

In this way the star bustled them out of her dressing-room, and the three men repaired to the front of the house. It seemed, indeed, that Zirknitz was inclined to leave them, but after a glance at the haggard face of Ellis he changed his mind. Cass invited him to sit at their table, which he did, and accepted a lemon-squash.

"I never take anything stronger," he said gracefully. "It is bad for the nerves; it makes the hand shake."

"I can understand that as applying to a doctor like myself, M. Zirknitz, but to you--how does it apply to you? What profession do you follow that requires nerve?"

"I play cards, doctor. I earn my living in that way; and, let me tell you, one who does so must have a steady hand, a clear brain, and nerves of steel."

As he spoke, Schwartz, all alone, strolled past. He nodded to the Austrian, but frowned slightly when he saw him with Ellis. Then pausing by the table, he tapped Cass on the shoulder with a plump, beringed hand.

"Mr. Cass, mine goot frend, vill you with me gome? I haf pisness with you that gannot wait."

"Is there money in it, Schwartz?"

The German cast another look at Zirknitz, who was trifling with a cigarette which he took out of a handsome silver case. "I dink zo," he said pointedly.

"In that case I'll come. Wait for me here, Ellis. M. Zirknitz, I wish you good-evening," and Cass went off in high spirits with the fat Schwartz, so that Ellis and the Austrian were left alone.

The table at which they were seated was placed at a comparatively secluded corner, out of the crush of people and the glare of the light. Yet, quiet though it was, Zirknitz, after a glance round, appeared to be annoyed by the position.

"Will you come to my box, monsieur?" he said, rising. "I fancy it is more comfortable there."

"But my friend Cass?"

"I shall instruct the waiter to bring him to the box when he returns here. Come, doctor," added Zirknitz, in a whisper, "I wish to speak with you--about the murder."

A thrill ran though Ellis as he followed the Austrian up the stairs. Was the man about to confess to his crime? That was hardly probable. Perhaps he intended to explain the cypher. Yet that, also, was doubtful. By this time Ellis had seated himself in a shady corner of the box. He was thoroughly puzzled, and could conceive of no reason why Zirknitz should seek this interview. The young man closed the door, removed his coat and hat, and offered Ellis a cigarette. The doctor refused on the plea that he had smoked enough, for he could not bring himself to accept anything from the hands of M. Zirknitz. They were those of a card-sharper, a swindler--a murderer! In this belief Ellis decided to let the Austrian do most of the talking, hoping to trap him--if not into confession at least into damaging admissions. His own *rôle* was to say nothing--to know nothing and to give M. Zirknitz a sufficiency of rope to weave a halter. The situation was uncomfortable, and Ellis felt as though he were dealing with a graceful but dangerous tiger which required dexterous and diplomatic handling.

"I am glad to meet you, doctor," said Zirknitz, in his quiet voice. "Indeed, had I not done so here by chance I should have called on you."

"With reference to the murder?"

"Say with reference to Mrs. Moxton and her husband's will. Also, monsieur, with reference to her husband's cousin. Ah, *scélérat!*"

"Busham?"

"Ah, yes, that is the name. Mr. Richard Busham, the advocate."

"Do you know him?"

"*Moi, monsieur? Non!* but I hope to know him if he does not behave well to my sister."

Dr. Ellis leant back in his chair with a gasp of astonishment. "Your sister!"

"Mrs. Moxton, or, rather, I should say, my half sister. Did you not know? *Quel dommage!*"

"How should I know?" muttered Ellis, not yet recovered from his amazement.

"Because my sister, Mrs. Moxton, told me that you were her best friend."

"I hope I am her friend. But I confess that I am astonished to hear that you are her brother. Are you not a foreigner?"

"Yes, to speak truly there is no blood relationship. Mrs. Gordon, the mother of my sister, married my father, Adolph Zirknitz, who was a widower. The marriage of our parents is the bond between us."

"I see. And you have two sisters?"

"*Oui!* Mrs. Moxton, who is Laura, and Miss Janet Gordon. Who told you?"

"Polly--Miss Horley."

"Ah," muttered Zirknitz, with a look of displeasure, "she talks so much, oh, so very much."

Here was a discovery. The mythical lover of Mrs. Moxton, the murderer of her husband, if the blood signs could be believed, turned out to be her brother by marriage. A queer sort of relationship truly, which Ellis had not met with before, still, one sufficiently close to put any question of love out of the case. If so, what was Zirknitz's motive for committing the crime? Ellis felt that he was floundering in deep water.

"Why do you tell me all this?" he asked suspiciously.

"Because Laura says that you are her friend, and will help her through with this matter."

"Of the murder."

"Partly, and of the will. Busham is not an easy man to deal with, and he is annoyed that old Moxton's money should go to Laura."

"How do you know it will go to her?"

"Laura told me she thought there was a will leaving it to her."

"M. Zirknitz," said Ellis, after a few moments of reflection, "will you answer a few questions?"

"Oh, yes, most certainly. I have much confidence in you, Dr. Ellis."

The other did not reciprocate this sentiment, but had sense enough to keep his doubts to himself. "You knew Moxton very well, I presume?"

"*Oui da!*" Zirknitz shrugged his shoulders; "but we were not friends. He was always drinking and quarrelling. I do not like such men."

"You disliked him?"

"No. I dislike no person. It is troublesome to do that."

"Did you visit him at Dukesfield?"

"I did not. He hated me, you understand. Sometimes at night I went to see my sister when all was quiet."

Ellis reflected that these visits must have been conducted with considerable secrecy, seeing that Mrs. Basket was ignorant of them; but, to be sure, they took place after dark. "Were you at Myrtle Villa on the night of the murder?"

"No," answered Zirknitz, coolly and promptly. "I thought of going for my sister Janet, but I changed my mind. Moxton was drunk, so I fancied he might make trouble."

"Then you saw Moxton on that night?"

"Oh, most certainly! He was--he was--" Zirknitz hesitated.

"He was in the secret gambling-room of Schwartz," finished Ellis, guessing his thoughts.

The Austrian's face became as blank as a sheet of white paper. "But I do not understand," he said with a shrug.

"Oh, well, as you please," returned the doctor, coolly. "I know nothing about the matter myself. To continue where we left off. Where did you see Moxton last on the night he was killed?"

"Oh, at the bar in there," Zirknitz was clever enough to take his cue; "he was drunk--not very bad--but noisy and troublesome. He drove away in a cab."

"Right down to Dukesfield?"

"That I do not know. I went home to bed myself."

This was a lie, as Ellis shrewdly guessed, but the Austrian carried it off with an air which showed that he was an adept at falsehood.

"When did you hear of the murder?"

"I saw it next day in the papers."

"Then why did you not go to Dukesfield to help Mrs. Moxton?"

"Why should I?" said Zirknitz, with a charming smile. "Murder is not pleasant. I don't like such things. And I might have got into trouble. I do not mind saying, doctor, that mine has been a life of adventure, and I care not for the police."

"You are afraid," said Ellis, wondering at the selfishness and brutal candour of the confession.

"*Certainement!* I am afraid. Oh, think badly of me if you like. I am so bad that I can be no worse. But I shall help my sister over the money."

"Because you hope to get some?"

"Eh! why not? I am extravagant."

Ellis felt a strong desire to kick this handsome, smiling rascal, but he doubted if even a kick would rouse any shame in him. The man seemed to have no moral sense; just such a soulless, brainless being who would commit a crime. The doctor began to look upon him as a psychological curiosity, and felt more convinced than ever that he had killed Moxton. The want of money supplied the motive.

"Who do you think murdered Moxton?" he asked, resolved to startle the man into a confession.

"Who do I think murdered Moxton," repeated Zirknitz, blandly. "Why, my dear Monsieur, I think Mr. Busham did."

Ellis jumped up. "On what grounds do you make such an accusation?"

"Ah, I will not tell you that now," replied Zirknitz, coolly. "I do not yet know you well. If Mrs. Moxton agrees I may do so."

"But if you will--"

"Oh, no, I tell nothing. See, the performance is over. We must go."

While the Austrian was reassuming coat and hat, Ellis felt sorely tempted to tell him about the blood signs and accuse him of killing Moxton. But as yet he had not sufficient evidence, and it was unwise to put Zirknitz on his guard until he could get him into a corner. Before he could decide, the Austrian nodded and, still smiling, slipped out of the box. Ellis stooped to pick up his stick and followed almost immediately, only to find that Zirknitz had vanished into the crowd. What his attitude was towards himself, the doctor could not quite determine. "I shall question Mrs. Moxton about her brother," he reflected, as he went in search of Cass.

The journalist was in the office of Schwartz, but came out when he heard Ellis inquiring for him.

"How did you get on with Zirknitz?" he asked, as they hailed a hansom.

"Oh, pretty well. He talked a great deal, and declared that Busham killed Moxton."

"The deuce! How can he prove that?"

"I don't know. He refused to give any proof, and cleared out before I could question him further. What did Schwartz want to see you about?"

"To warn you and me against cultivating Zirknitz."

"Is he a bad egg?"

"The worst in the nest, from all accounts. I believe he killed Moxton on his own hook."

"He denies that he was at Dukesfield on that night."

"Denies it? Like his brass. Why, he left this hall to take Moxton home."

"Who says so?"

"Schwartz."

"Do you believe Schwartz?"

Cass drew a long, long breath. "I don't know what to believe," he said. "All these men form part of the gang of rogues. There is more devilry in this case than we know of, Bob."

CHAPTER X
A STRANGE DENIAL

On arriving at their lodgings, both men were too excited over the case to feel inclined for sleep. Instead of going to bed, they made up the fire, lighted their pipes, and continued the discussion commenced in the hansom. It was then that Ellis repeated the statement of Zirknitz anent his connection with Mrs. Moxton and her sister.

"So you see, Harry, the man is Mrs. Moxton's brother, or half-brother--not her lover."

"He is really no relation at all," retorted Cass, rather amazed by what he heard. "Mrs. Moxton's mother married the father of Zirknitz, did she? That makes the young man brother by marriage, but so far as parentage and blood go, he could marry Mrs. Moxton to-morrow."

"I tell you the man isn't her lover."

"Possibly not, after what Zirknitz has told you--that is, if it is true. But he may be the murderer for all that."

"Oh, I agree with you there," said the doctor. "The creature is one of those selfish, soulless beings without moral feelings. So long as he could do so, without risking his neck, I quite believe he would go so far as murder. Then he is a spendthrift and a Sybarite; so to get this money it is just possible he killed Moxton. But if he is guilty, Mrs. Moxton does not know of his wickedness."

"Then why did she faint when his name was mentioned?"

"Because no doubt she is aware of his dangerous nature, and perhaps may think him guilty. What I mean is that, up to the moment I mentioned the name, she did not suspect Zirknitz."

"Humph!" said Cass, looking at the fire. "It might be so. What do you intend to do now? The situation is complicated."

"I will see Mrs. Moxton and tell her that I have met Zirknitz."

"Will you tell her also that he accuses Busham?"

"Yes! because from what he said, Mrs. Moxton may know the grounds upon which he bases his accusation."

"Then she must be inculpated in the crime," cried Cass, decisively.

"I don't see that," said Ellis, much annoyed. "Come what may, I believe that poor little woman is innocent."

"Because you are in love!"

"It may be so," assented the doctor, gloomily. "Love warps my mind, perhaps, but the whole case is so extraordinary and mysterious that it is difficult to say who is, and who is not, concerned in it."

"In my opinion the whole lot are concerned in it," said Cass, "and the desire for money is the cause of the crime. By the way, I asked Schwartz about the Gordon sisters."

"He knows both, I suppose?"

"Yes; but he praises only one--Janet Gordon. Mrs. Moxton he appears to think very little of."

"That may be because he does not know her so well. Janet was in the employment of Schwartz as a programme-seller and attendant, but Mrs. Moxton, being a typewriting girl, only occasionally visited the hall. In any case I admit that the Gordon girls appear to be shady."

"Yet you think of marrying one."

"I shall not do so if I find out anything wrong," said Ellis. "It is true that I am in love with Mrs. Moxton, but should her past be a bad one, I am sufficiently reasonable to crush down my feelings. Still, I believe that she is more sinned against than sinning; and it will be my task to solve the mystery of this murder--to prove that my belief is a true one."

"I am with you there, Bob, and I shall help you with all my heart. But I tell you plainly that Schwartz has no very good opinion of Mrs. Moxton. He declares that she is frivolous, vain and foolish."

"She is none of the three, Harry, believe me. And Janet?"

"Janet is staunch, honest, clever and honourable. Schwartz respects her highly, and he is not the man to bestow praise unduly."

"I should like to see this girl," said Ellis, thoughtfully, "particularly as she may throw some light on the murder. From the description of old Ike, I believe the woman he drove to Pimlico was Janet Gordon. She must know something or she would not have been crying on that night, nor would she have given up her situation at the Merryman Music-Hall so suddenly."

"Perhaps you consider her guilty?"

"No. On the authority of those signs on the arm of the dead man, I believe Zirknitz killed him."

Ellis rose and stretched himself. "We have a terrible tangle to unravel, Harry," he said after a pause.

"I don't see why we need trouble ourselves to do it, Bob."

"I do. Mrs. Moxton must be proved guiltless."

Cass shook his head. "Even if she is innocent of the murder her past is shady," he said. "She is not the wife for you, Bob."

"When the crooked is made straight we shall see about that, Harry."

With this confident assertion Ellis retired to bed, but not to sleep. In spite of his love, he could not but see that Mrs. Moxton's reputation was in peril. So much as he had gleaned of her past from herself and other sources was, to say the least of it, shady. The people with whom she had associated were scarcely reputable. Her husband had been a dissolute scoundrel, and Zirknitz, the so-called brother, was an idle vagabond, devoid of self-respect and morals. Then the sister! Schwartz praised her, but Schwartz was not overclean himself in character, and the employment of the girl at a second-rate music-hall was not the style of thing to recommend her to respectable people. Then, again, Mrs. Moxton's conduct was shifty and underhand. She declined to tell the truth, yet from the surrounding circumstances it was plain that she knew it. Taking these things into consideration, many a man would have cut himself off root and branch from the widow; but some instinct told Ellis that she was not so evil as she appeared to be, and made him anxious to sift the matter to the bottom. Therefore he got up in the morning still bent upon dealing with Mrs. Moxton and her doubtful past. After all, she might prove in the end worthy of an honest man's love.

Shortly after breakfast Mrs. Basket waddled in with the announcement that Mrs. Moxton was at the door. Ellis was surprised. This was the first time she had come to his house since the terrible night of the murder, and their first meeting since her fainting at the name of Zirknitz. The doctor hailed this unexpected visit as a good omen. If she were guilty, she would scarcely take such a step; and it might be that, weary of fencing, she had come to confess the truth.

It was with Judas-like affability that Mrs. Basket introduced the widow into the room. She believed in Mrs. Moxton's guilt. She wished to see that guilt made clear, and desired that it should be punished. Yet she smiled and gabbled, and was ostentatiously friendly until dismissed by Ellis. Mrs. Moxton breathed a sigh of relief as the door closed on the treacherous creature. She looked pale, but was as pretty as ever, and Ellis felt the charm of her manner sap the doubts he entertained of her honesty. At first he thought that she had come to explain about Zirknitz, but at the outset of the conversation Mrs. Moxton did away with this idea. Her opening remark revealed the reason of her call.

"I have found it, doctor," she said, producing a legal-looking blue envelope. "The will of Edgar is in this packet."

"Where was it hidden, Mrs. Moxton?"

"You will never guess. Under the matting of the sitting-room. I expect he concealed it there in one of his magpie-fits when he was drunk, and forgot its whereabouts when he got sober. This is the will, doctor, and it leaves all his property, real and personal, to me."

"So you are a rich woman, Mrs. Moxton," said Ellis, eyeing her gravely. "I congratulate you."

"Don't be in too great a hurry to do that," she rejoined coolly. "I have yet to reckon with Mr. Busham and his suspicions."

"You can disprove those, can you not?"

"I do not know; I cannot say. I must first learn what his suspicions are, and that will be easy enough. I have only to show Mr. Busham the will and he will come out with his accusation. Whether I can refute it remains to be seen; and it is for this reason that I wish you to visit the lawyer with me."

"Visit Mr. Busham?" said Ellis, considerably astonished at this unusual proof of confidence. "But what can I do?"

"Two things. Firstly, you can be a witness to the charges, which, I feel certain, Mr. Busham will bring against me."

"Then you trust me so far as to let me hear those charges?"

"I do, because in the face of all circumstantial evidence to the contrary you believe that I am innocent. For that reason I regard you as my friend, for that reason I ask you to stand by me in my time of trouble."

Ellis looked at her doubtfully, not knowing what to make of this speech, which, indeed, was puzzling enough. An honourable woman, entangled in the net of villains: a scheming adventuress, bent upon arriving at her own ends--Mrs. Moxton was one or the other; and the love which Ellis had for her inclined him to believe she was honourable. Still, there must have been some shadow of doubt on his face, for Mrs. Moxton became bitter and angry and unmeasured in speech.

"Am I mistaken in you?" she demanded sharply. "Have you repented of what you said to me the other day? Is it with you as with other men--words! words! words! If so, tell me, and I go--go never to trouble you or see you again. You must trust me in all or not at all."

The doctor was astonished at this sudden outburst, and hastened to assure Mrs. Moxton that she did him an injustice. "I firmly believe in your innocence, and I feel certain that you can explain away the charges against you."

"They have yet to be made, doctor," replied the widow, cooling down, "And when they are I wish you to be present. That desire will show you whether I can answer them or not. Another reason why I desire you to visit Mr. Busham in my company is that I am anxious for you to protect me from his violence."

"Confound the fellow!" cried Ellis, firing up. "Will he dare to lay hands on you?"

"Not on me, but on the will. If I defy Mr. Busham, he is quite capable of taking the will from me by force and destroying it."

"We shall see about that," said Ellis, after a moment's thought. "However, I guess from what you say that Busham is a tricky, shifty scoundrel. Certainly I will come with you, Mrs. Moxton. When are you going?"

"To-morrow morning. We can take the underground railway to Esher Lane."

"Very good. I will see you in the morning. In the meantime will you leave this will for me to look over?"

Ellis made this demand with the intention of seeing how far Mrs. Moxton would trust him, as it was scarcely fair that the confidence should be all on one side. To his secret astonishment and openly-expressed pleasure, she agreed at once to the request.

"As you trust me, I shall you," said Mrs. Moxton. "Keep the will by all means till to-morrow morning; but take care of it, as it is an original document."

"I will put it away now "; and Ellis locked the document up in a despatch-box which stood near his desk. "And I thank you for this proof of confidence, Mrs. Moxton; you will not find it misplaced."

"I am quite sure of that, doctor. I trust you thoroughly."

"In some ways, yes, in others, no. For instance, why will you not tell me about Zirknitz?"

Mrs. Moxton turned pale. "I cannot tell you about him--yet."

Ellis was vexed. "Well, there is no need," said he, a trifle crossly. "I know about this man."

"About Rudolph? About--"

"Yes, about your brother by marriage."

The widow, who in her excitement had half risen from her chair, fell back into it again thunderstruck. "Where did you meet him?" she stammered.

"At the Merryman Music-Hall."

"Do you know that place?" shrieked Mrs. Moxton, much agitated.

"I was there last night. There I met Zirknitz, and he told me of his relationship to you. Also," and here Ellis grew grave, "he informed me who murdered your husband."

Mrs. Moxton's capacity for amazement was exhausted by these repeated shocks, and she sat limply in her chair. The last remark, however, seemed to brace her up for the moment.

"And who does he say killed Edgar?" she asked, with an anxiety she strove vainly to conceal.

"None other than Busham, the man who--"

Mrs. Moxton interrupted him with a burst of hysterical laughter. "Dr. Ellis," said she, in a choking voice, "I *know* that is false. Mr. Busham did *not* kill my husband."

CHAPTER XI
A HALF CONFESSION

Mrs. Moxton made the statement regarding Busham's innocence with so much decision that Ellis looked at her in surprise. It was strange that she should defend a man she disliked. "How is it that you think him guiltless?" he asked anxiously.

"Because he is a coward, and too timid to kill a man."

"Your husband was stabbed in the back in the darkness. That looks like a coward's deed."

"All the same, I feel sure he is innocent," persisted the widow. "I can see no reason for his killing Edgar. He knew that old Moxton made another will shortly before dying, and that he would not inherit. No! look at it which way you will, Mr. Busham is not the murderer. I detest the man, but I must be just to him. What else did Rudolph tell you, or, rather, on what ground does he accuse Mr. Busham?"

"He refused to tell me the grounds without your permission."

"My permission! Why, I know nothing about the matter."

"From what Zirknitz hinted it would appear that you do," said Ellis, a trifle drily.

"Then he shall tell his story in your presence," rejoined Mrs. Moxton, quickly, "and you will see that I know nothing."

"I shall be glad to be convinced. Tell me, why did you keep silent about this young man?"

"Because of the blood marks on the arm of Edgar."

"Oh, so you knew the secret of the cryptographic signs, in spite of your denial?"

"I did! I do! As a matter of fact, I taught that cryptogram to my--" here Mrs. Moxton closed her mouth with the nervous gesture of one who thinks she is saying too much.

"To your sister," finished Ellis, quietly.

Mrs. Moxton fenced. "How do you know that I have a sister?"

"From the books in your house, some of which contain your name and that of your sister Janet. Also from a cabman on the rank here, who described to me a woman so like you that I am convinced she is your sister--possibly, from the exact likeness, your twin sister."

The widow became the colour of chalk at these words. "Where did the cabman see her?"

"He drove her to Pimlico on the night, and about the time, your husband was murdered."

For a moment or so Mrs. Moxton looked doubtfully at Ellis, and passed her tongue over her dry lips. The doctor could see that she trembled. His unexpected knowledge evidently inflicted a shock on her nerves. Yet, for all her emotion, she still strove to baffle his curiosity. "You seem to know a good deal about my husband," she said irritably.

"I do. Because I am anxious to clear your name and extricate you from a difficult position. Mrs. Moxton"--Ellis rose and bent over her with great earnestness--"why will you not be frank with me? You tell me much, but you will not tell me all."

She moaned and moved away from him. "Heaven help me, I dare not tell you all."

"Yet I am your best friend."

"I know it, but you would shrink from me did you know the truth."

Ellis took her hand gently. "Tell me who murdered your husband?" he whispered urgently.

"I don't know! I swear I don't know!" cried the widow, with much vehemence; "if I did I would tell."

"The blood marks hint at Zirknitz."

"Yes, yes, but I am sure he is innocent. Rudolph is foolish, vain, shallow, but he never killed Edgar, I swear."

"Yet the name on the dead man's arm?"

"I don't know the reason of that; I can't say why Edgar wrote it. I read it myself, although I denied all knowledge to you. It was for Rudolph's sake that I lied. I was afraid lest he should get into trouble. I asked him if he was in Dukesfield on that night, but he denies that he was."

"And your sister Janet?"

A tremor passed through the frame of Mrs. Moxton. "She came to see me on that night, and we quarrelled; she left before Edgar came back, and, I suppose, went crying down the road to take a cab home."

"Did she see the murder committed?" asked Ellis, tentatively.

"I don't know," said Mrs. Moxton, under her breath. "I am--oh," she burst out, "I can't tell you more. I have had to do with villains and rogues all my life, and I am paying the penalty of their sins, not of my own. I have tried to be a good woman, so do not shrink from me. I swear that I do not know who killed Edgar. Some day I may tell you more, but at present I cannot--I cannot."

She hastily let down her veil and stood up to go. "You trust me still? you believe in me yet?" she said entreatingly, and with tears.

"I do," replied Ellis, touched by her emotion. "You puzzle me more than I can say, yet I am sure you are innocent of all evil. But if you would only tell me--"

"Some day! some day!" she interrupted hastily; "but not now. Yet what you should know, you shall know. Come to me between four and five to-day, and you will meet Rudolph. He shall confess what he means by hinting at my knowledge of Mr. Busham's guilt."

"I will come with pleasure, but do you think Zirknitz will come?"

"Yes. I will telegraph for him now. He loves me and trusts me, and I have great power over his weak nature. In my hands he is like wax, and if the truth is in him you shall hear it this afternoon. But I know that Rudolph is innocent. I am certain that Mr. Busham did not strike the blow. Heaven alone knows the secret of Edgar's death. Good-bye, good-bye, Dr. Ellis, and do not think badly of me. Indeed, indeed, when the moment comes I can put myself right in your eyes. What other people say or think, I do not care, but you must be shown that I am more sinned against than sinning. Good-bye!" She stretched out her hand, and withdrew it abruptly ere he could touch the tips of her fingers. "Not yet, not yet," she muttered, and swiftly glided from the room before Ellis could recover from his surprise.

This woman was more inexplicable than ever. Apparently she knew a great deal, as could be seen by the information which Ellis had dragged out of her. Yet she refused to be candid, although at the same time she admitted that she wished to preserve her friend's good opinion. The hints dropped in her last hasty speech showed Ellis that he was right in trusting to his instinct concerning her nature. Whatever Mrs. Moxton might be,--mysterious, shady, dangerous,--she had a straightforward, honest mind. It was warped by the circumstances in which she found herself placed through no fault of her own, and she was forced to fence and lie, and act a tricky part for some strong reason which she refused to impart to Ellis. Privately he thought that all her energies were bent upon shielding her sister, as formerly she had striven to shield Zirknitz by denying all knowledge of the cryptogram. Could Janet Gordon be the guilty person? Ellis twice or thrice asked himself this question, but could find no answer to it. Her hasty flight on the night of the murder, her tears, her silence, her absence from the music-hall hinted--if not at personal guilt--at least at guilty knowledge. If she did not kill Moxton herself,--and on the face of it she could have had no reason to do so,--she must have seen the crime committed. Perhaps she had met with the assassin face to face, and had fled horror-struck and weeping to the cab-stand. The way to learn the truth would be to see her. No doubt she had confessed the cause of her terror to Mrs. Moxton, and it was this secret which Mrs. Moxton, loyally doing violence to her nature, wished to conceal. But if the widow would not speak, Ellis made up his mind that Janet Gordon should; therefore he resolved to find out the number of her lodging in Geneva Square, and call upon her. Failing Mrs. Moxton, Zirknitz might supply the information. In her own despite Mrs. Moxton must be rescued from the dangers which appeared to surround her. She had confessed with less than her usual caution that she was paying for the sins of others, and Ellis was bent upon bringing the truth to light and making the actual sinners suffer for their own wickedness. The fact that he was more deeply in love than ever, greatly assisted him in arriving at this conclusion. Yet a wise man, a worldly man, would have called him a fool to still love and trust Mrs. Moxton in the face of all he knew about her. But in this instance instinct was stronger than argument, and Ellis was satisfied that the woman he loved would yet emerge vindicated and spotless from the dark cloud of troubles which obscured her true nature.

Precisely at half-past four he presented himself at Myrtle Villa. The door was opened by Mrs. Moxton herself. Apparently she had been watching for his arrival, and Ellis, guessing as much, felt his heart swell with joy. Strange that his love at this moment should move him to emotion.

"Rudolph is here," whispered the widow. "Let me question him. I know how to make him speak out."

Ellis nodded, and when ushered into the sitting-room was sufficiently composed to meet Zirknitz with a smile. The Austrian looked an Adonis in the daytime, and was admirably dressed in a smart frock-coat, fawn-coloured trousers, and patent leather boots of high polish. He was a modern

D'Orsay in looks and dress--just the handsome kind of scamp to attract silly women. Ellis had no doubt that one day or another Monsieur Rudolph would pick up an heiress, and become respectable. The young man was shallow and selfish, yet--if one could judge by his smiling face--harmless enough in other ways.

"I am delighted to see you, doctor," said the Austrian, blandly. "You must forgive me for leaving you so abruptly the other night. But you were beginning to ask me indiscreet questions, so I--vanished."

"Rudolph always considers himself first," observed Mrs. Moxton, who was making tea. "He is the most selfish creature in existence."

"The most selfish!" assented Zirknitz. "I think of no one by myself. Why should I? *Quelle bêtise.*"

"Every man should think of others!" said Ellis, hardly knowing what to say in the face of this cool confession.

"Oh, *mon cher* monsieur, that doctrine is out of date. Thank you, Laura. I will have some tea. Three sugar bits, my dear. I love sweets, and sunshine, and pretty girls--as a butterfly should."

Mrs. Moxton looked at the pretty youth with something of contempt. "You need not blazon forth your follies, Rudolph. I know what you are; and Dr. Ellis will soon find you out. What is this story you have been telling him about me?"

"Story? None! What is it, monsieur? *Point de moquerie!*"

"You accuse Busham of this murder!"

"Ah, yes, now I remember; and I refused to tell you my reasons until permitted by my sister. Have I your consent, *ma chère* Laura?"

"Tell everything you know," cried Mrs. Moxton, with a frown. "Why you should bring my name into the matter I don't know. There is no need for you to explain, Rudolph; you will only romance. Why do you suspect Busham?"

Zirknitz looked at Ellis. "Can I speak freely?" he asked doubtfully.

"Certainly. The doctor is my best friend."

"Ah! so charming to have a best friend. Hear, then, monsieur, and you, my dear Laura. When I was at Dukesfield on the night Edgar was killed--"

"Why," said Ellis, with something of anger in his tones, "you told me you were not at Dukesfield on that night."

Zirknitz shrugged his handsome shoulders. "I told a lie! Oh, yes, I always tell a lie when necessary. I did not know Laura wished me to speak, so I told what was not true. What would you, monsieur? Your questions were indiscreet. My answers were false. *Voila!*"

"Never mind excusing yourself, Rudolph. What about Mr. Busham?"

"Eh, my dear sister, I believe he killed our poor Moxton! Why not? I saw the excellent Busham in Dukesfield on the night of the death."

CHAPTER XII
MR BUSHAM, SOLICITOR

Lounging in his chair, Zirknitz made this astonishing statement as though it were the most natural thing in the world. Mrs. Moxton looked at Ellis in surprise, and both looked at Rudolph.

"Is this true?" asked Ellis, doubtfully.

"Eh, *mon cher*, most assuredly. I tell lies only when necessary."

"Rudolph, you must explain how it was you came to be in Dukesfield on that night."

"My dear sister, did I not say I would come for Janet?"

"Yes, and you never kept your promise."

"No," chimed in Ellis. "Polly Horley said the same thing."

Rudolph smiled in a most engaging manner.

"Ah, that excellent Horley! How much she knows of what she knows not. My sister, have I your permission to smoke?"

Mrs. Moxton impatiently nodded an assent. "But I am waiting to hear how you did not come for Janet and yet were in Dukesfield on that night."

With great deliberation, Zirknitz selected a cigarette from his silver case and lighted it before making any reply. Selfish in his every act, he offered none to Ellis--an omission which troubled that gentleman very little. He had no great love for this egotistical butterfly.

"My Laura," said Rudolph, blowing a whiff of smoke, "on that night I was playing cards in the *salon* of the music-hall, and I won twenty pounds from Edgar. He had not the money, but he gave me an 'I O U.' Then, most furious at his loss, he drank and drank till he was as a wild beast. I was going for Janet, and at the station I saw our Edgar; but to avoid him I went in another carriage. At the station of Dukesfield, I tried to run from him; but he saw me and followed; *quelle bêtise*. There was trouble, and he wished to fight. So when he went home I saw it was foolish to come for Janet, as Edgar would be raging. I took back another train, and a cab to my rooms in Bloomsbury. *Voila*, the story!"

"Not all the story!" said Ellis. "You have left out the most important part--about Busham."

"Ah, that dear Busham. When Edgar was angry with me on the platform of the Dukesfield station, I see out of my eye's corner that clever advocate. He was watching our dear Edgar, but did not come near him. I knew him. Oh, yes, I knew his face very well."

"I did not know you were acquainted with him, Rudolph!"

"Best of sisters, I do not tell you all I know, or do. Our Edgar one day took me to see the excellent Busham in his office, where they did fight. Oh, I tell you, monsieur, the good Busham sent us away with a flea in our ears. Edgar spoke of his father, and said that Busham was a rogue wanting the money; so we had trouble, and we left very enraged. So I met Busham, the pig," finished Zirknitz, smiling, "and I do not forget his face."

"He was watching Edgar on the night of his death?"

"*Oui da!* He thought I saw him not, but I did see him. *Ma foi*, I have quick eyes, Laura, as you well know. He ran out of the station after Edgar, and I am certain followed to kill him."

"About what time was this?"

"On eleven. I did hear the clock of the station strike when I was enraged with Edgar."

"And Moxton was drunk?" inquired Ellis, anxiously.

"He was straight drunk, for he could walk; and cross-drunk, assuredly, since he wished to fight with me. But I care not for boxing," said Mr. Zirknitz, gracefully. "And I go home to bed before twelve of the clock, like a good little boy. Aha, monsieur, you think I kill Edgar, do you not? *Eh bien!* You demand of my landlady if I was not in my bed before twelve of the clock. I did not kill our poor Edgar. Why should I when he owes me twenty pounds? *Cher* Ellis, you are in the wrong box."

"You had better wait until I accuse you before excusing yourself," said Ellis, drily. "But even with this story of Busham having been at Dukesfield, I do not see how you can be certain of his guilt."

"Eh? To me it appears clear. This clever Busham wanted the money of his uncle, and murdered Edgar to get it."

"But, Rudolph, at that time Mr. Busham knew that a second will had been made."

"Most certainly, *chère* Laura. If no second will had been made, this excellent Busham would not have killed Edgar."

"We can say nothing for certain until we see Busham," said Ellis, after a pause, "but there is one thing probable, Mrs. Moxton. If Busham accuses you in any way we can turn the tables on him."

"You call on Busham, Laura."

"To-morrow. I must see about the will."

"And the money," smiled Rudolph. "Eh, *ma s[oe]ur*, forget not the most important thing."

"To you, perhaps, not to me," replied Mrs. Moxton, with contempt. "My object is to get free of all this trouble."

"Of course. I will help you; eh, most certainly. But ask me not to meet the police. I do not like the police. For if--"

"Monsieur Zirknitz," said Ellis, cutting short this speech, "how came it that your name was indicated on the dead man's arm?"

The Austrian was in no wise discomposed by this remark. "Ah, Laura spoke to me of that. I do not know; I cannot say. But I think, ah, *ma foi*, I think."

"What do you think, Rudolph?"

"My sister, I quarrelled with your good husband at the Dukesfield Station, and he went away enraged with me. When Busham struck him in the back--"

"You can't be sure of that," interrupted Ellis, impatiently.

"Eh, but I am sure," insisted Zirknitz, politely; "and Edgar, not seeing who stabbed him so cruelly, thought that I did so. Then he wrote on his arm to tell Laura."

"But why in cryptographic signs?"

"That I cannot say. The sign of a lizard was always the good Edgar's little jest on me. For my name is that of a town in my country where there are many lizards. Edgar found it in a book and always jested. Very little jests pleased the good Moxton. But now I must go," said Zirknitz, rising. "I have told you all you wish. My sister, do you desire me to speak more? No! My good doctor, have you a policeman without for my arrest? No! Ah, then I will take my leave. Not *adieu*, dear friends, but *au revoir*."

When Zirknitz sauntered out of the room, Mrs. Moxton looked after him with a singular expression. "What do you think of him?" she asked.

"He is clever. It is a great pity he does not put his talents to better use."

"Oh," Mrs. Moxton shrugged her shoulders, "I don't ask you about his character. I know about that well enough. But do you think he is speaking the truth?"

"Yes. He has no reason to tell a lie. I daresay he did see Busham."

"And do you think Mr. Busham is guilty?"

"I can't say. We have not sufficient evidence to go upon."

Mrs. Moxton turned the conversation abruptly. "Did you read the will?"

"Yes. I see that all the money is left to you. I will give you back the document to-morrow. What time do you wish me to call?"

"About eleven o'clock. I have written to Mr. Busham making an appointment for mid-day. I am glad you are coming with me," said the widow, sighing; "it will be a difficult interview."

"That remains to be seen. At any rate, we are not so defenceless as we were before. If Busham accuses you--although I don't see on what grounds he can do so--we can denounce him on the evidence of Zirknitz."

"He will deny that he was at Dukesfield."

"Zirknitz can swear to his presence."

"No doubt, but will Rudolph do so? He is so afraid of the police."

Ellis reflected for a moment. "You are not so candid with me as you might be, Mrs. Moxton," said he, seriously, "therefore you render my task the more difficult. But answer me truly now. Has Zirknitz ever done anything for which he is wanted by the police?"

"Not to my knowledge," replied the widow, frankly, "but he is such a coward, and his life is so open to danger, that the very name of the law terrifies him beyond expression. It is for this reason that I am certain of his innocence, and for the same reason I shielded him by feigning ignorance of the cryptogram. But we can talk of these things later. I am tired now."

In this abrupt way she dismissed Ellis, and he left the house sorely puzzled, his constant state of mind in reference to Mrs. Moxton. If he did marry her he would marry the sphinx. That was clear enough.

Mr. Richard Busham inhabited a dingy set of offices in Esher Lane, adjacent to the Temple. His staff of clerks consisted of two under-fed, overworked creatures, who scribbled in an outer room for dear life at a miserable wage. The inner room, which had two dusty windows looking on to Bosworth Gardens, was occupied by their employer. This apartment was piled all round the walls with black tin boxes with the names of various clients painted on them in white. A brass-wired bookcase contained a few calf-bound volumes of legal lore; there was a large table covered with green baize, two chairs, and--nothing else. A more dreary or barren room can scarcely be conceived, but Mr. Busham being a miser, it suited him well enough. He called himself a lawyer, but he was really a usurer, and gained a handsome income by squeezing extortionate interest out of the needy. If the walls of Busham's private apartment could have spoken they would have protested frequently against the sights they were compelled to witness. The Holy Inquisition tortured people less than did this rat of a lawyer. He ground down his victims to the lowest, he lured them into his spider-web, and rejected them only when he had sucked them dry. His law was a farce, his money-lending a tragedy.

The man himself resembled in looks Fraisier, the rascally lawyer so admirably drawn by Balzac in "Le Cousin Pons." Like Fraisier, Busham was small, sickly-looking and pimpled; his expression was equally as sinister, and his heart as hard--that is if he had a heart, which his clients were inclined to doubt. He scraped and screwed, and swindled, and pinched to collect all the money he could; yet what benefit he thought he would gain from this hoarding it is impossible to say. He never spent it, he lived like a hermit, like a beggar, and gratified his sordid pride with the knowledge that he was becoming a wealthy man. And when he arrived at wealth? What then! Busham never gave this consideration a thought, perhaps because he fancied he would never become as wealthy as he wished to be. Altogether the man was an unwholesome, evil creature, who should, for the good of humanity, have been in gaol. But he was clever enough to keep on the right side of the law he so misinterpreted.

At mid-day Mrs. Moxton and Ellis presented themselves before this engaging being, and looked round the frowsy office with disgust. Another chair had to be brought in from the outer room for the accommodation of the doctor, and when his visitors were seated, Busham welcomed them with a nervous titter, which showed that he was not quite easy in his mind regarding the interview. Indirectly he resented the presence of Ellis.

"Well, Mrs. Moxton," said he in a whistling whisper, his usual voice, "is there a will?"

The widow produced the blue envelope and laid it on the table. "There it is," she said, "it leaves all the property to me."

Busham went green and gasped, "All the property to you!" He snatched up the will and hastily read it over. "I see it does," was his answer; then after a pause he cast an evil look on Mrs. Moxton, and opened a drawer of his desk. Evidently he was about to bring forward his accusation.

"Since you have shown me the will, I have something equally interesting to show you," said he, quietly. "What do you think of this, Mrs. Moxton?" And on the table he laid a bone-handled carving-knife, on the blade of which were dull, dark stains of blood.

CHAPTER XIII
MRS MOXTON'S SURRENDER

The widow turned pale when she saw the knife, and, unable to speak, looked at Ellis. The doctor understood that pleading glance and at once threw himself into the breach. "Where did you get this?" he asked Busham, sharply.

The lawyer, scenting an enemy, looked mistrustfully at the speaker out of his rat's eyes. "Your pardon, sir, who are you?" he demanded, with a kind of snarl in his voice.

"I am Dr. Ellis, who examined the body of Moxton. I am also the friend of Mrs. Moxton, and I came here to assist in this interview."

"And suppose I refuse to allow you to assist?"

"In that case, I shall know how to account for your possession of that knife."

Busham gave a kind of screech, and threw himself halfway across the table, shaking with anger. "You dare to insinuate that I killed my cousin?" he asked, in a whisper.

"Why not; you were with your cousin on that night."

"It is a lie!"

"It is the truth!" cried Mrs. Moxton, finding her voice. "Rudolph saw you following Edgar from the station."

"And who is Rudolph?"

"Monsieur Zirknitz, my brother."

"Another of your shady gang. I dare you to--"

"Speak more civilly," interrupted Ellis, starting up, "or I shall twist that lean neck of yours."

At once the innate cowardice of Busham became apparent. Shaking and white, he dropped back into his chair, terrified at the doctor's angry look and menace. Yet, withal, he could not curb his venomous tongue.

"Violence," he gasped. "You do well, Mrs. Moxton, to bring your bully here."

"What! You will have it!" cried Ellis, angrily.

Busham flung himself out of his chair, and shot up one of the dirty windows. "Another step and I call the police," he whispered.

"Do so, and I shall give you in charge."

"Me in charge, and for what?"

"For killing Moxton. You were with him shortly before his death."

With a scared look Busham drew down the window and returned to his desk. "I am safe from your violence I hope?" he said, looking apprehensively at Ellis.

"So long as you are civil to Mrs. Moxton I won't touch you," replied the doctor, coolly, and in his turn sat down.

"He! he!" laughed Busham, nervously rubbing his hands, "it will be as well to conduct this interview quietly."

"I think so," observed Mrs. Moxton, with an expressive glance at the knife, "for your own sake."

"Say rather for yours, Mrs. Moxton."

"What do you mean?"

"He! he! that will take some time to explain. If you would rather be alone with me--"

"Alone with you," repeated the widow, in tones of disgust. "I would rather be alone with a serpent. Dr. Ellis shall stay--at my particular request."

"Dr. Ellis has no intention of leaving," remarked that gentleman, and folding his arms relapsed into a grim but observant silence.

Busham, with a vexed air, scratched his chin with one lean finger. "As you please," said he, with apparent carelessness, "but he will not think much of you when I tell all."

"You know nothing about that," retorted Mrs. Moxton, very pale, but in a steady voice, "and I have come here to learn all. Of what do you accuse me?"

"All in good time, dear lady," said Busham, harshly. "This knife was found by me in your garden, on the morning I called to see you after the murder."

"Are you sure you did not find it there on the previous night?" asked the widow, sneering.

"I was not in the garden on that night."

"Neither was the assassin," interposed Ellis, quickly. "Moxton was stabbed as he stepped in at the gate."

"Or as he turned to close it," retorted Busham, smartly.

Mrs. Moxton held her handkerchief to her mouth and shivered, but with her eyes on Busham's mean face nodded to him to continue. The man, seeing that she had a vague terror of his threats, did so with a chuckle. "Since you know that I was at Dukesfield on that night," he went on, "I admit it. Why should I not? I am innocent and can prove as much. So Monsieur Zirknitz saw me? H'm! I know that scamp; no one better. He called here one day with my cousin to extort money on the plea that I had undue influence over my uncle, but I soon turned the rascals out, I can tell you. I am a dangerous man when roused." Mr. Busham chuckled, and repeated the phrase with relish. "A dangerous man."

"Oh, I daresay," said Mrs. Moxton, with a contemptuous air, which accorded ill with her pale face and uneasy manner. "Dangerous as a fox, or a stoat, or a weasel may be. You belong to the vermin tribe, you do."

"Go on with your story, man," directed Ellis, curtly.

"Civil, civil, oh, very civil," snapped Busham, "but I'll teach you both manners before I'm done with you. At Dukesfield was I? Yes, I was. He! he! do you know what I saw there, Mrs. Moxton? You don't. Well then, I'll tell you, and take this for my fee."

"The will!" gasped Mrs. Moxton, as Busham clawed the document. "I thought that was what you wanted."

"Leave that will alone," growled Ellis, scowling.

Mr. Busham immediately pushed the paper away. "It will come back to me soon," said he, nodding. "Oh, I know, I know."

"What the deuce do you know? Speak out, can't you?"

"Softly, Dr. Ellis, softly, all in good time. Maybe you won't be so pleased with my knowledge when you are possessed of it."

"I am the best judge of that; go on. You were at Dukesfield on the night of August 16th?"

"Yes, I was," cried Busham, with sudden energy. "I received intelligence of my uncle's death, and knowing that a new will had been made, that Edgar was the heir, I wished to inform him of the good news. From that scamp, Zirknitz, I learnt that Edgar went night after night to the Merryman Music-Hall in Soho, so I sought out that place in the hope of seeing him. I did see him," sneered Busham, "and, as usual, he was drunk--not in a fit state to talk business. When he left the hall to go home I followed his cab in another, thinking that the fresh air would sober him. But at Charing Cross underground station he had two more drinks, and, more intoxicated than ever, stumbled into a carriage. I went into another, thinking it best to see him home lest he might come to harm."

"You were very solicitous for the safety of one who had robbed you of a fortune," said Ellis, with a cynical look.

"That's just it," cried Busham, slapping the table with the open palm of his hand, "he was to get the money, and I wished to gain his good will, and take what pickings I could. Half a loaf is better than none, isn't it? If Edgar had lived I would have got the money--somehow. Even you, Mrs. Moxton, would not have prevented that."

"Even I," repeated the widow, bitterly. "Heaven help me, I would have been the last person to prevent your robbery. I never had any influence over Edgar. Go on, Mr. Busham. Did you succeed in ingratiating yourself with my husband by announcing the good news of his father's death?"

"No, I didn't," snarled the lawyer. "I saw him quarrel with Zirknitz on the platform of the Dukesfield station, and then I watched him leave."

"Not only watched him, but followed him," said Ellis.

"Yes, I wanted to see how he would get home. I tried to speak to him, but being drunk he swore at me, and struck out with his cane. Seeing that there was no good to be got out of him in his then state, and that it would be useless to tell him the news, I resolved to defer the appointment until the morning, when I hoped to find him sober and repentant. He went away. I did not follow, but remained for some time talking to a policeman. Then I missed my train, and as I had to get home, made up my mind to take a cab."

"An unusual expense for you," jeered Mrs. Moxton.

"Oh, I wouldn't have taken the cab if I could have walked," said Busham, naïvely, "but I was not strong enough to do so. All the cabs at the station had carried away the theatre people, and I went down the road to the cab-rank in the middle of Dukesfield. There was one cab there. But just as I turned the corner a woman came running down the road and jumped into it. She was crying, and trembling and wringing her hands. I saw her face in the light. It was you, Mrs. Moxton."

"One moment," said the widow, as Ellis was about to contradict this preposterous statement. "I never saw you until after the death of my husband, and you never saw me. How, then, did you recognise me?"

"Oh, that was easy. Edgar gave me your picture."

"I should not have thought that Edgar was sufficiently friendly with you to do that."

"He was when I lent him money," said Busham, quietly.

"Why did you lend him money?"

"Because several times he called on me and threatened to see his father. I did not want him to do that lest he should be forgiven, so I lent him money on condition that he did not go. Uncertain of what his reception would be, he took my bribe and stayed away. On one of those occasions he showed me your photograph, Mrs. Moxton."

"Edgar was forgiven after all," said the widow, ignoring this last remark.

"Yes, but the forgiveness did not do him much good. He! he!"

"Mr. Busham!" burst out Ellis, who could no longer be restrained. "You did not see Mrs. Moxton enter a cab on that night. The lady was her sister."

"I know about the sister," said Busham. "The twin-sister. Zirknitz told me."

"Are you friendly with Zirknitz?" asked Ellis, with unconcealed surprise.

"Very!" retorted the lawyer, with an ugly grin. "I lend him money."

"Lend money to a scamp like that, whom you hate, who will never repay you?"

Busham scratched his chin. "Oh, as to that," said he, "I know what I am about, you may be sure. So it was your sister, Mrs. Moxton? Bless me, how like she is to you; a twin, of course? I see. Why was she crying and flying?"

"She may have cried because we quarrelled on that night," said the widow, in an agitated tone; "but she was not flying. She merely went home."

"To thirty-two Geneva Square, Pimlico? I know! I know!"

"How do you know?"

"Because I picked up another cab and followed her!"

"Why did you do that?"

"I thought she was you, and wished to know where you were going at that hour of the night. Your sister going home? Ah, that explains it."

"So far, so good, Mr. Busham," said Ellis, weary of this talk; "but what about the knife?"

"I called next morning at Myrtle Villa, after hearing of the murder. I searched the garden for traces of the criminal, and found that knife hidden behind some laurel bushes."

"It was not hidden," cried Mrs. Moxton. "It was thrown there by Edgar."

"Ah! you acknowledge that the knife is your property," said Busham.

"Why should I deny it? That knife is ours. It was tossed into the garden by Edgar."

"And this is rust on it, no doubt," said the lawyer, touching the stains. "Not blood, then, Mrs. Moxton?"

The widow rose with an agitated face, and, snatching up the will, thrust it into Busham's hand. "Take it, and say no more," she said harshly.

"Mrs. Moxton! The will!" cried Ellis, jumping up.

"Let him destroy it! Let him take and keep the money!"

"Thank you; and in return I will hold my tongue. If you like you can take the knife," said Busham.

Mrs. Moxton picked it up, thrust it into the pocket of her cloak, and, without a glance at the amazed doctor, left the room. As she did so Busham stepped across to the grate in which a starved fire was burning and deliberately placed the will on the coals. Before Ellis could prevent it, the document was ablaze, and shortly nothing remained but black tinder.

"Now," snapped Busham, pointing to the door, "you can follow her."

CHAPTER XIV
THE PIMLICO HOUSE

Having seen Busham commit a felony by burning the will, Ellis left the office. He did not even protest against the destruction of the document, since it was none of his business to do so. Mrs. Moxton, who benefited under the will, had not only handed it over to her enemy, but had advised him to destroy it. She had exchanged it, so to speak, for the knife with which Moxton had been killed, and, in addition, had secured the lawyer's silence by yielding up her property. Silence about what? That was the question Ellis asked himself, and which he put to Cass when reporting the extraordinary scene which had taken place in the Esher Lane office.

"I think I can guess what Busham hinted at," said the reporter. "He accuses Janet Gordon of the crime?"

"Why should he? She had no motive to kill Moxton, so far as I can see."

"Precisely, so far as you can see, Bob. Depend upon it, Busham is certain that Janet Gordon is guilty, and Mrs. Moxton knows that such is the case, else she would not give up her property so freely."

"You mean that she allowed the will to be destroyed so that Busham should not accuse her sister?"

"Yes. All along I said that Mrs. Moxton was shielding some person; now we know who the person is."

"It might be so," said Ellis, reflectively. "Janet Gordon may have rushed out of the house with that knife and have killed Moxton, and afterwards she may have ran weeping to take a cab from so perilous a place. But why did she stab the man? Why? Why?" and Ellis, according to custom, began to pace the room.

"Ah," said Cass, who was resting on the sofa, "you must ask Mrs. Moxton for a reply to that question."

"She won't reply to it. For some reason which I cannot fathom she persistently keeps me in the dark."

"H'm!" mused the journalist. "A dangerous, secretive woman! Don't get your back up, Bob, I am not calling her names. But you must admit that she is secretive, and secretive people are always very dangerous to those of a more open disposition. But how did Mrs. Moxton excuse herself for letting Busham burn the will?"

"I don't know, Harry. I have not seen her since she left the office with that knife concealed in her pocket."

"What! Did she not wait for you outside?"

"No," replied Ellis, gloomily, "there was not a sign of her, although I searched all round. What is queerer still, she has not been home since. I have called twice at Myrtle Villa this afternoon, but no one is there."

"Queer. I wonder what she is up to. After all, Bob, the burning of the will does not amount to much. Mrs. Moxton, as the dead man's widow, retains half the money. Busham has not got the whole."

"No, but he will get it," said the doctor, vehemently. "He'll not keep silence in spite of her giving up half. He will blackmail her into giving up the whole by threatening to betray her sister."

"You forget. By burning the will he has committed a felony. If Mrs. Moxton is clever she can checkmate him with that."

Ellis shook his head doubtfully. "I think not, Harry. She might get him put in prison; but then, in revenge, he could hang her sister. No, Busham is all right on that point; he would not have burnt the will had he not known how to protect himself."

Cass stared at the ceiling and mused for a few moments. "From what you tell me of Zirknitz," he said at length, "I am not inclined to trust that man. He is too thick with Busham, and, moreover, he is a venal creature who would sell any information for money."

"Do you think he is in league with Busham?"

"I would not put him on so high a plane. I think he is the tool of Busham, though. I should not be at all surprised to find the whole of this mystery traced to that Esher Lane office."

"What! Do you think that Busham is guilty?"

"No; he is too clever to risk his neck."

"Zirknitz?"

"No; the Austrian is a coward."

"Then what do you mean?"

"I hardly know how to explain," said Cass. "I fancy old Moxton's money is at the bottom of all this business, and that Busham is the moving spirit. Watch him, Bob, he is the clue to the mystery."

"H'm! I don't know. He is too crafty for me to tackle directly, but I might get at his secret through other people. The person to question, Harry, is Janet Gordon. Mrs. Moxton evidently thinks her guilty, and to save her surrendered the property. Now, I wish to see the girl personally and judge for myself."

"Mrs. Moxton won't speak out."

"Hitherto she has refused, but in the face of the destroyed will she may do so. I shall question her closely when I next see her."

"You are still firm in your belief about her honesty?"

"Yes; and I still love her," said Ellis, firmly. "Depend upon it, Harry, when the truth comes to light, Mrs. Moxton will not be to blame."

"Humph!" said Cass. "I hope so, for your sake, since you are so bent upon making her your wife. But I tell you one thing, Ellis, the widow won't show herself again to you in a hurry."

"Why not?"

"Because, like Zirknitz, she will not risk your indiscreet questions. She has gone away to avoid answering them. My opinion is that she will remain away."

For the next few days the arrest of events in connection with the case seemed to point to a realisation of this prophecy. Mrs. Moxton did not return to Myrtle Villa, and it remained shut up and empty. Dr. Ellis called at least once a day, but on no occasion did he find the widow within. From the time she vanished so suddenly from Busham's office, he never set eyes on her. Firm as was his belief in her innocence, Ellis began to have his doubts about her absolute rectitude. Why had she vanished? Why did she remain away from her best friend, as she considered him to be? Whither had she gone? Ellis wondered if he could trace her, but, after consideration, decided in the negative. There was no clue to her hiding-place. She had disappeared as a drop of water in a mighty ocean. Failing in his attempt to trace the widow, Ellis made up his mind to follow another clue. For this purpose, four or five days after Mrs. Moxton's disappearance, he sought out number thirty-two in Geneva Square, Pimlico. Here, according to Busham's statement, he expected to find Janet Gordon.

Everybody in London knows Geneva Square. It obtained an unpleasant celebrity in connection with the tragedy of the Silent House, and was given as a sketch in many weekly papers at the time of the murder. The Silent House is pulled down now, and its position occupied by a brand-new mansion of red brick, which, amongst the sober grey houses of the square, looks like a purple patch on a ragged cloak. Number thirty-two was in the corner of the square, and from the notice in the window Ellis saw that it was a boarding-house. On inquiring for its mistress, a sluttish servant introduced him into a tawdry drawing-room, where he found himself in the presence of a lean, yellow-faced woman, overdressed and effusive in manner. At one time of her life Mrs. Amber--such she informed him was her name--must have been very pretty, but the years had turned her into a lean and withered hag on the wrong side of forty. She wore a gaudy pink tea-gown, trimmed with cheap black lace, and carried on wrists and neck a considerable number of jingling ornaments, inexpensive and showy. For the sake of her faded beauty the window-blinds were drawn down, and Ellis found himself in a kind of subdued twilight. Mrs. Amber was affected and garrulous, but, on the whole, did not appear to be an ill-natured woman. She seemed to have a high opinion of Janet Gordon.

"Dr. Ellis!" said she, disposing herself in a graceful attitude in a basket-chair. "Do you wish to see me with a view to becoming a lodger?"

"No, madam. I have come to inquire for Miss Gordon."

Mrs. Amber raised her painted eye-brows--they were painted, although the obscurity of the room prevented that fact becoming too apparent. "You are a day after the fair, doctor," said Mrs. Amber, with an artificial laugh. "I regret to say that Miss Gordon has left us."

"Left this house?" said Ellis, astonished at this information.

"Three days ago she left us. Her sister came for her and took her away. I am very sorry Miss Gordon is gone; I always had, and always shall have, the highest opinion of Miss Gordon. Of course, she was not the kind of person with whom I have been accustomed to associate," added Mrs. Amber, arranging the bracelets on her lean wrists, "being only an attendant at a low music-hall. Still, she was thoroughly respectable, and a thorough lady, I will say that. You wonder, perhaps, Dr. Ellis, that I should have a lodger of that occupation. But I am liberal in my views I was on the boards myself many years ago. You must have heard of the beautiful Miss Tracey, who appeared in the burlesque of 'Cupid,' at the Piccadilly Theatre--I was Miss Tracey. I was Cupid, and I retired only when I married Mr. Amber. Ah!" sighed the ex-actress, "he is dead now, and I keep a boarding-house. Such is life!"

As soon as Ellis could cut short these biographical reminiscences he did so. "I am sure that Miss Gordon is all you say, madam," he observed politely. "But can you tell me where she now is?"

"No," replied Mrs. Amber, promptly, "I can not. Her sister came for her. She packed her box and they left the house. She gave no address to the driver of the cab. Mrs. Moxton simply told him to go to the Marble Arch. I was out at the time Mrs. Moxton arrived, and she went straight up to her sister's bedroom. I was glad that I returned before Miss Gordon went away."

"Why do you say that?" asked Ellis. "Did you not see her daily?"

Mrs. Amber glanced round apprehensively. "I wouldn't say it to everybody," said Mrs. Amber, giving a queer reason for her confidence, "but as you are a stranger it does not matter. Since that horrid murder of poor young Moxton, Miss Gordon has been very strange. She came back from seeing her sister on the night of the crime, and from that time until she left, remained shut up in her room."

"Shut up in her room?"

"Yes. Was it not strange? In vain I wished to see her. She refused to let me into the room. Sarah, my servant, took up her meals and told me that Miss Gordon was in bed the whole time. Through the door, and by sending a message with Sarah, I implored her to have a doctor, but she refused constantly. Yet when she went away she did not look so ill as Mrs. Moxton. Ah!" said Mrs. Amber, expressively, "she looked ill if you like."

"Strange!" murmured Ellis. "I suppose you knew the Moxtons intimately?"

"Very intimately. Laura Gordon lived here before her marriage, and she was married to Edgar Moxton from this house. It was terrible that he should have been killed in so savage a manner, Dr. Ellis. I never liked Mr. Moxton; but I must say I was horrified when I heard of his doom. I wonder who killed him?"

"That is what I and many other people would like to know," said Ellis, drily. "I suppose you guess from my name, Mrs. Amber, that I am the doctor who examined the body?"

"Yes. I guessed that when I received your card, and was certain of it when you asked for Miss Gordon. You know Miss Gordon, of course?"

"No, I never set eyes on her."

"Really! Then why do you wish to see her?" asked Mrs. Amber, anxiously.

"To see if she knows anything about this murder."

Mrs. Amber did not reply immediately, but trembled so violently that her ornaments jingled like so many little bells. "Dr. Ellis," said she at length, in a shaking voice, "you speak the doubts that are in my own mind."

"What! Do you think she knows of the murder?"

"I am unwilling to harm Miss Gordon," said Mrs. Amber, in a scared tone, "as I have a great respect for her. But I fancy she must have seen something on that night or she would not have shut herself up in her bedroom all these weeks. And, Dr. Ellis, do you know I have sometimes suspected her myself."

"Of the murder?"

Mrs. Amber nodded. "I was afraid of getting into trouble if I spoke," she said nervously, "and I really can't bring myself to believe that, Miss Gordon killed her brother-in-law. But Sarah brought down a pair of cuffs to be washed--Miss Gordon's cuffs--and they were spotted with blood!"

CHAPTER XV
WHAT MRS. AMBER KNEW

Mrs. Amber made this communication in a whisper, and then drew back to see what effect it would have on Ellis. He appeared to be less surprised than she expected, for the scene in Busham's office had prepared him to suspect Janet Gordon. Therefore he was not astonished to find his suspicions confirmed, but he did not go quite so far in his accusation as Mrs. Amber.

"For reasons which I need not repeat," said he, deliberately, "I am not so surprised as you expect me to be. I have long thought that Miss Gordon might know of the murder, but I most emphatically decline to believe that she struck the blow herself."

"But the cuffs were stained with blood. I washed them myself, and told Sarah to hold her tongue."

"Miss Gordon may have handled the body after the death, Mrs. Amber, but I do not think she killed the man. If you read the report of the evidence I gave at the inquest you will remember that I stated no woman could have struck so firm and sure a blow. I hold to that opinion. Moxton was stabbed by a man."

"What man?"

"That is what I wish to ask you, Mrs. Amber."

The ex-actress turned pale beneath her rouge, and two red spots glowed crudely on her white cheeks. "I!" she exclaimed, drawing back. "How do I know who killed Mr. Moxton?"

"I do not say that you know, but from your experience of the man, and from a certain amount of knowledge which you must have of his past life, it is not improbable that your suspicions may have fallen on someone who had a grudge against him."

"No," declared Mrs. Amber, vehemently. "I suspect no one--that is, I *did* suspect Miss Gordon because of those blood-stained cuffs. But from what you say she cannot have struck the blow, so I can guess at no one else. If I had done so I should have come forward to give evidence. It was my personal liking for Miss Gordon which made me hold my tongue. Besides, I never saw the cuffs until the inquest was over and Moxton was buried," finished Mrs. Amber, naïvely.

"You have known Mrs. Moxton and her sister for some time?"

"For four years, more or less. They are twins, you know, and very much alike, but I think Janet the cleverer of the two. Certainly she has the finer character, and the more generous spirit. Laura is fickle and vain."

Ellis did not agree with this, and, being in love with the Laura aforesaid, was vexed to hear such deprecatory criticism. However, he consoled himself with the hackneyed reflection, weak in so clever a man, that women never spoke well of one another, and continued his inquiries. "Mrs. Moxton earned her money by typewriting, did she not?"

"Yes. Janet wanted to keep her out of mischief, so selected that employment as the best for her. Laura wished to be an attendant in the Merryman Music-Hall, also, but this Janet would not allow."

"I wonder the sisters could not obtain better employment."

"My dear Dr. Ellis, they were wretchedly poor and had to take what they could get. Anything to earn their bread and butter."

"Where did they come from?"

"I don't know. They came to me recommended by Herr Schwartz, and I took them in as cheaply as I could, because I fancied Janet's face. Ah, me," sighed Mrs. Amber, "I trust I have not been mistaken. But so good a girl! No! in spite of those cuffs I believe in her still. Why, Dr. Ellis, Janet is worth a dozen of her sister or that scampish brother."

"Zirknitz, do you know him?"

"Yes, I do," replied Mrs. Amber, bluntly, "and I don't like him. He was here with the girls for some weeks, and let them slave and work while he idled about. He left pretty soon, as I remonstrated with him on the subject, and I wasn't sorry to see his back."

"You know Schwartz also, it seems."

"Of course. I was in a theatrical company of his once," cried Mrs. Amber, with great vivacity. "Papa Schwartz is a dear, good man. He helped Janet by engaging her at the hall. She was his private secretary."

"I thought she sold programmes?"

"Oh, yes, and showed people to their seats. She did that also, but she really was the secretary of Papa Schwartz. Sometimes Laura went to the hall, and it was there she met Moxton. He fell in love with her and married her. She brought her pigs to a pretty market," said Mrs. Amber, vigorously but vulgarly, "but she would marry the beast in spite of all that Janet could say."

"Do you know about Captain Garret?"

"And Hilda? Of course I do. They lived with me for some time. Poor girl, she is blind, and Papa Schwartz is devoted to her."

"What about her father?"

Mrs. Amber shrugged her shoulders and jingled her bracelets. "Oh! he is well enough," said she, in a disparaging tone. "A broken-down military dandy. Hilda would be in the workhouse so far as he is concerned. It is Papa Schwartz who keeps them both."

"In spite of his reputation Schwartz seems to be a good man," said Ellis, musingly. "You say that he engaged Janet Gordon as his private secretary. How was that?"

"He knew her in Germany, or Austria, or somewhere."

"Indeed, have she and her sister lived abroad?"

"Yes, for a considerable time, I believe. Their stepfather was a M. Zirknitz, as I learnt from that horrid Rudolph. But I really do not know anything about their past life, doctor. Janet held her tongue, and so did Laura, in spite of her frivolity. Who they are or where they came from I do not know. Papa Schwartz might."

"I shall see him about it. There appears to be some mystery about these girls, Mrs. Amber."

"I agree with you, doctor. But I am certain they are ladies."

"Did you see Miss Gordon when she arrived here after the murder?"

"No, she came in after midnight and used her latchkey. I thought nothing of it at the time, as her business kept her out late. But when I wished to see her about the murder, which was in the morning papers, she refused to let me enter the room. I never saw her until two or three days ago, when she went away."

"Did Mrs. Moxton come to see her?"

"No, Mrs. Moxton never came near her, except this last time to take her away. Where they have gone I know no more than the man in the moon."

"Did anyone come to see her while she was in her bedroom."

"Papa Schwartz did, but she refused to admit him."

"I wonder if he will know their whereabouts?"

"He might," said Mrs. Amber, with a nod. "Janet is his secretary."

"She was, but she is not now," contradicted Ellis. "She gave up her place."

Mrs. Amber's face expressed unqualified amazement. "Dear me, how does she intend to live?"

"I don't know. Mrs. Moxton may keep her."

"But Mrs. Moxton hasn't a shilling. Her husband's father disinherited him for marrying her."

"Oh, she will come in for some of the property," said Ellis, trying to explain without mentioning about the burnt will. "Old Moxton died intestate, so half his estate will go to his son's widow. But tell me, Mrs. Amber, do you know a man called Busham?"

"No, I never heard the name."

"He did not call here?"

"Not to my knowledge. Who is he?"

"Mrs. Moxton's lawyer." Ellis rose to take his leave. "Well, Mrs. Amber," he said, "I am much obliged for the information you have given me. For certain private reasons I wish to find out who murdered Moxton, but it seems you cannot help me."

"No, I know of no one. I cannot guess who would be such a villain. But if anyone knows, it will be Janet Gordon. She must have handled the body, as those blood-stained cuffs show."

"You knew that she was at Dukesfield on that night?"

"Yes, she told me she was going, and that M. Zirknitz intended to fetch her home. That was why I wished to see her next day when the papers were full of the murder. I thought she might know something about it. And I am sure she does know," cried Mrs. Amber; "else why did she shut herself up in her room all these weeks? I wouldn't have stood it from anyone but Janet Gordon, I can tell you."

"You appear to have a great admiration for her."

"I have. Women, Dr. Ellis, do not as a rule admire one another, but when I know how Janet Gordon has protected that silly sister of hers, and looked after her scampish brother, I think of her as one of the noblest women I have ever met."

With this eulogy bestowed, in the opinion of Ellis, on the wrong woman, Mrs. Amber parted from him with theatrical effusion. The doctor left the

Pimlico house in a musing frame of mind. It was strange that Mrs. Amber, who seemed to be a good-natured woman in spite of her many affectations, should think so little of Mrs. Moxton. Ellis piqued himself upon being a reader of character, and he could not bring himself to believe that he was mistaken in the widow. But he was puzzled to think how completely Mrs. Amber's estimate of her nature differed from his own. Thinking about Mrs. Moxton recalled his mind to the fact of her disappearance and he wondered if Schwartz would know of her whereabouts. With this in his mind he hailed a hansom and drove to Soho. In the meantime, pending the discovery of Mrs. Moxton, he dismissed all speculations concerning her from his mind. So far as he could see, time and association were needed to explain her very complex character. After the interview with Mrs. Amber, the doctor considered the little woman more of a sphinx than ever, and he wanted her to speak and unravel the enigma of her being.

Schwartz was in his office when Ellis sent in his card, and saw the doctor at once. He looked more than a trifle careworn, but his pleasure in seeing Ellis was great, and he advanced towards him with outstretched hands. Nothing could have been more genial than his welcome.

"Aha, mine goot doctor," said he, in his guttural voice, "dis is kind to gome and zee me. But you haf not peen to zee mine Hilda. Dat is wrong."

"I have been very busy, Mr. Schwartz, but I will pay you a visit next week--say on Thursday afternoon."

"Ach, dat is goot. At what time, for I must be in mine house when you zee the eyes of mine poor Hilda."

"Four o'clock on Thursday next," said Ellis, booking the visit. "Oh, yes, I know the address. Goethe Cottage, Alma Road, Parkmere."

"Dat is zo, doctor. I vill wait you on that day. And what did you wish to zee me about?"

"Mrs. Moxton. She has left Dukesfield, and I wish to learn where she is."

The fat face of the German lost its genial expression. "Ach, she haf gone. Vell, and why do you gome to me, doctor?"

"I have been told that you are an old friend of Mrs. Moxton and Miss Gordon."

"Zo! Who told you?"

"Mrs. Amber, of Geneva Square, Pimlico."

"Ach, she was in a gombany of mine. I know her. Vell, yes, I am a frent of Miss Corton, but she haf left me. I do not know vere she is now."

"Has she not seen you lately?"

"Not, not des many veeks. And Mrs. Moxton haf gone?"

"Yes, she called at Pimlico for her sister, and they went off together."

"Why do you want to finze zem?"

"Because I have something to tell Mrs. Moxton."

"Zo! About ze murder of dat boor man?"

"Well, not exactly, but Busham, the--"

The eyes of Schwartz suddenly flashed with rage. "Ah, he is a pig, zat man. I could kill him."

"Do you know him?"

"Ach, I knows him. I did throw him out of mine music-halls. Vell, vell, do not talk of him, or I vill be angry. If you wish to know of Mrs. Moxton zee Zirknitz."

"Will he know?"

"I zink zo. If he does not, no one vill."

With this information Ellis was obliged to be content, but as he left the hall he observed that the German looked after him with a very singular expression.

CHAPTER XVI
ANOTHER MYSTERY

The behaviour of Schwartz perplexed Ellis, and during his homeward journey he pondered over the meaning of that glance. Could it be possible that the German was lying; that Janet Gordon had seen him, and had confessed what she knew of the crime? Ellis did not know what to think, but he was satisfied that the woman could solve the mystery. But she was not to be found; she had vanished as suddenly as Mrs. Moxton, and it seemed as though both of them were keeping out of the way lest they should get into trouble. But Ellis was bent upon discovering them at all costs.

In order to achieve this necessary purpose he kept a close watch on Myrtle Villa for the next few days, but all in vain. The house remained empty, and Mrs. Moxton gave no sign of reappearing. Ellis advertised judiciously in the *Standard*, but no notice was taken of his advertisement; he waited impatiently for the post, but no letter arrived. Mrs. Moxton and her sister had vanished as completely as though the earth had swallowed them up. The anxiety began to tell on Ellis's health, and Harry Cass advised him to abandon his pursuit of these shadows. As an intimate friend, Cass was brutally candid.

"It is no use mincing matters, Bob," said he, "the widow never loved you, and has made use of you only to secure her own ends. She will never return to Dukesfield."

"She must, Harry; if only to take the furniture out of her house."

"Oh, I daresay she will delegate that office to Zirknitz. There is no doubt that Janet Gordon knows the truth about the murder, and has confessed it to Mrs. Moxton. That is why both women are keeping out of the way."

"Zirknitz," repeated Ellis, paying no attention to the latter part of this speech. "I quite forgot about him. He may know where they are?"

"If he does he will not tell."

"I'll see about that, Harry. To-morrow I shall call on Zirknitz."

Cass shrugged his shoulders, but said no more. The obstinacy of Ellis was not to be overcome by argument, so, like a wise man, the journalist did not waste his breath in futile protestations. Secretly he was pleased that Mrs. Moxton should have voluntarily taken herself out of the way, as he did not wish Ellis to marry her. But in his own mind he was satisfied that the widow herself had proved by her last action that there was little fear of such an alliance taking place. To gain her own ends she had feigned a passion for Ellis; now that she saw nothing further was to be got out of him she had put an end to a disagreeable situation by disappearing. And this--in the opinion of Cass--was the end of Mrs. Moxton and her shady doings.

The next day Ellis went to see Zirknitz, the first thing in the morning, as he hoped to catch him before he left home. He knew that the Austrian was the most indolent of men, as Mrs. Moxton had told him as much, so it was unlikely that he would find him out of bed before ten o'clock. The doctor presented himself at the Bloomsbury lodging shortly before eleven, and found that even at so late an hour Zirknitz had not shaken off his slumbers. A smart maid-servant conducted him into an elegantly-furnished sitting-room, and took in his card. Shortly she returned with a message that M. Zirknitz in ten minutes would be at the disposal of his visitor. Like its owner, the room was very pretty. Wherever Zirknitz got the money to pander to his luxurious tastes, he certainly knew how to spend it. Ellis marvelled at the luxury by which he was surrounded, and wondered in what shady way it had been obtained. The walls were hung with Japanese silks of marvellous design and colouring, the floor was covered with a velvet-pile carpet of pale green, with a pattern of primroses. Green silk curtains draped the windows; there were charming pictures in every corner, and the furniture--also of pale green--was in the best possible taste. Near the window stood a piano, opposite to it a satinwood bookcase filled with French novels, and everywhere articles of useless luxury, evidently bought merely for the sake of buying. While Ellis was wondering at this bachelor's paradise, which more resembled the boudoir of a pretty woman, M. Zirknitz, fresh and pink from his bath, appeared through an inner door. He wore a loose dressing-gown of blue silk, and looked wonderfully handsome, if a trifle effeminate. With a joyous air he advanced to greet his visitor.

"*Cher ami*, so you have found me out. Well, I am charmed to see you, doctor. Is that chair comfortable? Good. Try this cigarette, it is a new brand. Can I offer you any refreshment--No? Ah, you are wiser than the majority of Englishmen. They eat and drink too much; bad for the nerves, pardy. Over-eating, over-feeding. *Quelle bêtise.*"

Zirknitz ran on thus lightly, but kept a sharp eye on his visitor, as he was anxious to know what had brought him there so early in the morning. Having fulfilled the duties of hospitality, he waited for Ellis to explain himself, which the doctor did almost immediately.

"I have called, M. Zirknitz, to inquire if you can inform me of the whereabouts of Mrs. Moxton?"

"Eh? How should I know? Am I my sister's keeper? Is she not in Myrtle Villa, Dukesfield?"

"No, she has not been there for five days. Your sister Janet has disappeared from Pimlico also."

"How do you know that, my brave doctor?" demanded Zirknitz, mockingly, yet with a shade of anxiety in his manner.

"Because I called there. Mrs. Amber informed me that Mrs. Moxton had taken away Miss Gordon. She did not know whither they had gone. I thought you might have had some idea."

"I fear, monsieur, I cannot assist you. I have not seen Mrs. Moxton since that day you spoke to me at Dukesfield. My sisters leave me much to myself. Why do you wish to see them?"

"I have my reasons," said Ellis, stiffly.

"And they are connected with that murder. *Mon cher* Ellis, *soyez tranquil*. I do not want to penetrate your secrets. I do not know where mesdames my sisters are. If I did I should tell you most assuredly, in spite of your bad opinion of me. But I am pleased you have come." Here M. Zirknitz rose and touched an electric button. "You will hear from my landlady that I was here on the night our dear Edgar was killed."

"I don't want any evidence to prove that, M. Zirknitz. I am satisfied that you are innocent."

"*Bon*. But there is a doubt in your suspicious English mind which peeps out of your eye. Ah, here is Jane. Jane," addressing the smart servant, "will you be so kind as to tell Mrs. Pastor I wish to see her at once. A pretty girl, Jane," resumed Zirknitz, as she vanished. "I like pretty women and all pretty things. You think my rooms nice, eh?"

"Charming. But I did not know you were so rich."

"Rich! *Ma foi*, I am as poor as a mousie mouse. If you--"

Before the Austrian could explain the source of his domestic magnificence his landlady entered the room. She was a formidable-looking woman, as tall as a Guardsman, with a severe face and the glance of a predatory bird. Dressed in black, with a lace cap and lace apron, she presented a wonderfully dignified and stately appearance. Anyone more unlike the scampish, airy Zirknitz it would have been impossible to conceive, yet the relaxing of her iron visage and the softening of her eagle glance showed that Mrs. Pastor was under the spell of her lodger's charm of manner. He greeted her with a sunny smile when she entered, and pointed to a chair, but Mrs. Pastor tacitly refused to be seated, and continued to stand bolt upright in the doorway.

"*Chère madame,*" said Zirknitz, in his most caressing tone, "this is Dr. Ellis, of Dukesfield, who examined the dead body of my brother-in-law, Mr. Moxton. He wants to know at what hour I returned here on the night of August 16th last, the night of the murder."

"Is it possible, sir, that you suspect Monsieur Zirknitz in any way?" asked Mrs. Pastor, solemnly, addressing herself to Ellis.

"No, I do not. M. Zirknitz is performing a little comedy for his own satisfaction."

"*Eh bien,*" said Rudolph, with a graceful wave of his hand, "then for my own satisfaction, madame, tell this dear doctor what I ask."

"Monsieur Zirknitz returned here at a quarter to twelve," said Mrs. Pastor. "I was still out of bed, and I admitted him myself. Next morning, when we were informed of the murder, M. Zirknitz begged me to take note of the time."

"Most assuredly," broke in the Austrian, impetuously, "for evil people might have accused me of the murder, since I was at Dukesfield then. But you see, my brave Ellis, I was here before twelve. As monsieur, *mon beau frère,* met his fate by your own showing about half-past eleven, I must be innocent."

"I quite believe in your innocence," said Ellis, rising. "There is no need to convince me so thoroughly. Thank you, M. Zirknitz, for the trouble you have taken in proving your case. Since you know nothing of the whereabouts of your sisters, my errand here is at an end. I shall go now."

"Ah, I am sorry to lose you. *Je suis désolé, mon bon ami.* Another cigarette? No? Good-bye. *Au revoir!* Some day we shall meet again. Mrs. Pastor, may I ask you to conduct monsieur, *mon ami,* to the door."

The landlady bowed solemnly, and, leading Ellis from the society of this graceful babbler, dismissed him with a second bow into the street. And in this unsatisfactory way ended the doctor's visit to the Austrian. Unsatisfactory, because he had obtained no information save that Zirknitz was innocent of the imputed charge, a conclusion at which Ellis had long since arrived. That same evening, after supper, he informed Cass about the alibi, but found that the journalist was less ready to accept the information.

"I don't trust Zirknitz," said he, emphatically, "neither does Schwartz. The man is a bad egg. I believe this murder is a family affair to get money.

Zirknitz, I daresay, murdered Moxton with that knife. Janet saw him do so, and told Mrs. Moxton, and they have both disappeared so that they may not be asked questions likely to lead to their brother's arrest. As for Busham, now that the will is destroyed he will hold his tongue."

"But the *alibi*," protested Ellis. "If Zirknitz was at Bloomsbury before midnight, he could not have been in Dukesfield at half-past eleven."

"The *alibi* may be a false one."

"You would not say so if you saw the witness to its truth. Mrs. Pastor is a regular Puritan, as rigid and unbending as a piece of iron."

"Yet she tolerates that frivolous scamp?"

Ellis shrugged his shoulders. "All women have their weaknesses," said he. "However, the main point is, that Zirknitz could not inform me of his sisters' whereabouts."

"Humph! Would not, rather than could not, I should say," observed Cass, crossly. "I don't believe myself that you will see Mrs. Moxton again, and I fervently hope that such will be the case. You have now one or two patients, Bob, the nucleus of a good practice, so give up this wild-goose chase after the widow and settle down to your work."

Before Ellis could answer this friendly appeal, which was made in all good faith, Mrs. Basket entered with a note for Ellis, which had been brought that moment by a boy. "Clark, the grocer's son," explained the fat landlady. "I 'ope, doctor, it's a noo patient, for if ever a gent deserved the sick and ailing, you are that gent," after which expression of sympathy Mrs. Basket waddled out of the room with much noise.

"Great heavens!" cried Ellis, who was reading the note.

"What is the matter, Bob?"

For answer Ellis threw the note to Cass on the sofa, and he read it also. Then the two men looked at one another in amazement. And well they might be amazed, for the note, inviting Ellis to call at Myrtle Villa, was from no less a person than Janet Gordon.

"Why should she write to me?" asked Ellis, on finding his tongue.

"Mrs. Moxton must have told her about your friendly spirit. Perhaps she wishes to confide in you, and her sister has brought her to Myrtle Villa for that purpose. Shall you go, Bob?"

"Go? I should think so. To-night I may learn the secret of the murder," and Ellis, putting on hat and coat, immediately left the room in a great hurry.

He ran rather than walked to Myrtle Villa, and, to his joy, saw a light in the sitting-room window. Mrs. Moxton, the woman he loved, had returned, and Ellis could hardly restrain his joy when the widow herself opened the door to him. After greetings, hurried and brief, were over, she conducted him into the sitting-room. At once Ellis looked round for the writer of the note.

"Where is your sister?" he asked.

"She is in the next room. You will see her soon. But you are making a mistake, Dr. Ellis. I wrote that note asking you to call."

"You? Good Heavens! Then you are--"

"I am Janet Gordon. It is my sister who is Mrs. Moxton."

CHAPTER XVII
A LIFE HISTORY

To say that Ellis was amazed by the discovery that the pseudo Mrs. Moxton was really Janet Gordon, would be to give a feeble idea of his feelings. For some moments he was too thunderstruck to speak, and remained staring at Miss Gordon as though she were a ghost. Seeing this, the girl--for she was no more--gently took his hand and guided him to a comfortable chair by the fire. Then she sat down at his elbow and explained herself seriously. She was as pretty as ever, but her cheeks were pale, there were dark circles under her eyes, and she had the nervous, agitated manner of one suffering from a great strain.

"Yes, I am Janet Gordon," said she, with a sigh, "and I have been masquerading as my sister ever since the terrible night of her husband's murder. My reasons for so doing you shall learn later on, for I am determined to tell you the whole truth of this matter so far as it is known to me."

"This is the secret you have been keeping from me?" said Ellis, much agitated.

Miss Gordon nodded. "I was afraid to speak before, even to so good a friend as yourself. But I find that I can bear my burden no longer; so I turn to you for help and comfort. You must aid me, you must see after my unhappy sister who lies in the next room."

"Is she guilty of the murder?" asked the doctor, rather harshly.

"No, no," cried Janet, trembling. "She is innocent, although appearances are against her. You will hear her story about that night from herself, but first I intend to relate my life history. I do not wish you to have a wrong opinion of me, Dr. Ellis."

"I could never have that, Miss Gordon," said Ellis, promptly. "I always believed that you were more sinned against than sinning. I wonder I did not guess at your identity before. Schwartz and Mrs. Amber both spoke highly of you, and I could not reconcile their opinion of Mrs. Moxton with what I knew of you under that name. Your explanation makes all clear."

"How do you know Mrs. Amber?"

"I went there to see the supposed Janet Gordon, and Mrs. Amber told me that you--that is Mrs. Moxton--had gone."

"I was afraid to leave my sister there after what Busham said," replied Janet, with a troubled air. "I let him burn the will, so that he might hold his tongue about Laura, for I saw that he suspected her. I took Laura to Bayswater, where we lived quietly for the last few days. But she is ill, and seeing no way out of the difficulty, and being in want of money, I resolved to bring Laura here and ask for your help."

"It will be freely given, I assure you."

In spite of the gravity of the situation, Ellis looked at his companion with so meaning a gaze that her cheek flushed and her eyes dropped before his. Yet she raised a deprecating hand to quell his emotion. "No, no, not yet, perhaps never. You must hear my story before you can think of me in that way."

"I shall always think the same of you. You are the dearest and the noblest of women. But I must confess that I am anxious to hear your confession. Begin at once; I am all attention."

Janet folded her hands on her black dress and looked musingly at the fire. There was a shadow on her resolute face cast by some bitter memory of the past. Ellis watched her in silence, and noted with pity how weary and worn she looked. Her reverie continued for two or three moments. Then she raised her head and related her unhappy past in quiet, melancholy tones.

"Laura and I are twins," she began. "We are very much alike in looks, but entirely different in disposition. I am strong-minded and calm; she is frivolous and highly excitable--indeed, sometimes I think she is not in her right senses, so furious are her rages. She has the fiery Celtic nature inherited from our mother, who was a Highland woman. I am more like my father, who was a calm-tempered, persevering man. We were born in Edinburgh, where my parents lived for some years after their marriage. My father was a doctor, and made a great deal of money."

"How strange that I should be a doctor also," said Ellis, meaningly.

Janet smiled and shook her head at the interruption. "As I say, my father made a great deal of money," she continued, "for he had a large and increasing practice, but a chill he contracted while visiting a patient in the country carried him off when Laura and I were ten years old. My mother was left a widow and well off, so taking a dislike to Edinburgh after her husband's death, she travelled abroad. For some years we wandered on the Continent, and Laura and I were educated at several schools, but my mother so wished to keep us beside her, that I am afraid we gained little knowledge. However, we learnt to speak French, German and Italian, so we benefited in some degree by our roving. For some years things went on like this, until at Carlsbad my mother met with Colonel Zirknitz, who was in the Austrian army."

"Rudolph's father?"

"Yes. Rudolph was then eighteen years of age, Laura and I fifteen. My mother fell in love with Colonel Zirknitz, and hearing that she was rich, he married her. But I am sure that he never loved her. We went to Vienna and lived there for some time. Our stepfather was not unkind, and treated my mother with every courtesy, but he was a gambler and a spendthrift."

"I see. The vices of Zirknitz are hereditary!"

Janet sighed. "I suppose so," said she, "but you must not be too hard on Rudolph, doctor. His failings are hardly vices. He has many good qualities."

"Mostly negative qualities, I fear, Miss Gordon. You are fascinated by that splendid scamp, like everyone else."

"That may be. Rudolph has not a fine character, and I have rather a contempt for him. All the same I am fond of him, although sometimes I feel angry for being so. Of course, Rudolph grew up with me, so to speak, and I look upon him as a brother. He was always wild; he has never done anything all his life, and although I have great influence over him I cannot get him to settle down."

"Is Colonel Zirknitz alive?" asked Ellis, anxious that she should proceed with her story.

"No, he died some time ago, but lived long enough to spend all my mother's fortune."

"And is she dead also?"

"Yes, she is dead," sighed Janet. "She died six months after her husband. I believe the loss of him broke her heart. He was a singularly fascinating man."

"After seeing the son I can well believe that. What happened when you found yourself alone in the world?"

"I came back to London with Laura. We were left penniless in Vienna, but Rudolph procured money somehow--by gambling, I fancy, and came to England with us. We left him in London staying at Mrs. Amber's house in Geneva Square, and went to Edinburgh to see if our father's relations would help us. Alas! they would do nothing."

"So much for the world's charity," said Ellis, cynically. "Brutes! what made them refuse, or, rather, what excuse did they make?"

"The excuse that my mother had married a second time. I begged and implored them to help Laura, if not me, but as they refused we came back to London. Rudolph behaved very well, for he paid our board at Mrs. Amber's for some time; so you see, doctor, he has some good points."

"I suppose so," replied Ellis, grudgingly. "He could do no less. Then you met Schwartz, I suppose?"

"We did. Some years ago in Germany we knew him, and on hearing of our penniless condition he gave me first an engagement as an attendant, and afterwards made me his private secretary. He offered to take on Laura also as an attendant, but I knew how frivolous she was, so I got her a situation in a typewriting office instead. I might have saved myself the trouble of protecting her from harm," sighed Janet, wearily, "for look what she has come to."

"Why did she marry Moxton?"

"She was tired of poverty and work. Moxton was the heir to wealth, and he professed to love her deeply. Against my will she married the man. I think she was encouraged by Rudolph, who fancied Moxton, as a brother-in-law, would lend him money. But after the marriage took place Edgar had no money to lend. His father resented the marriage, and cut him off with a shilling. With what money he had inherited from his mother Edgar went abroad with my sister. He gambled and drank, and treated Laura cruelly, as he accused her of being the cause of his ruin. They came back to England, and lived in this house the life I described at the inquest in the character of Mrs. Moxton."

"Ah," said Ellis, "now you come to the crucial point. Why did you impersonate your sister?"

"To save her from arrest and perhaps from death," replied Janet, feverishly. "I knew she could not face the inquest, or protect herself, and knowing that few people in this district were acquainted with her looks, and being very like her myself as her twin-sister, I seized the advantage offered, and stepped into her shoes."

"You are a brave and noble woman, Miss Gordon. So all through these terrible months you have been fighting on your sister's behalf?"

"Yes; she could not fight for herself. Rudolph, of course, knew the truth and supported me. Do you not remember how he called me Laura when you met him here?"

"I remember," replied Ellis, drily. "He never faltered or hesitated once. I think the young man has a positive genius for intrigue. But now that we have arrived at this point, Miss Gordon, I should like to know what really happened on that night."

"I will tell you all I know," said Janet, frankly, "then you shall see Laura and hear her story." She paused for a moment and continued in rapid tones: "I came here on that night to pay a visit to Laura, as I knew that Edgar would be at the Merryman Music-Hall as usual. I found Laura in a state of nervous rage against her husband, as he left her at home night after night, kept her short of money, and was altogether cruel to her. Laura, as you must know, doctor, has a neurotic temperament, and when angered lets her temper carry her beyond all bounds. She inherited this disposition with her Highland blood from our mother, who was likewise given to these fits of causeless rage. Often and often I implored Edgar not to anger Laura, knowing how dangerous she was when roused. But he neglected my warnings, and the pair were always fighting. I declare, doctor, that a dread of what might occur kept me in so nervous a state that I grew quite ill. I came down here constantly to soothe Laura, and never remained absent for any time without expecting to hear of a tragedy."

"I know the kind of irresponsible being your sister is," said Ellis, "and I do not wonder you were terrified. So the tragedy happened at last?"

"It did, and on that night," answered Janet, much agitated. "But it is not as you appear to think, doctor. Laura did not kill her husband."

"What about the carving-knife?"

"Oh, Edgar was killed with that, without doubt. What was said in Dukesfield about Laura carrying the knife was true. She was afraid of tramps in her half-hysterical state; and whenever a ring came to the door after dark she never opened it without arming herself with the knife. In this way she confronted the telegraph boy who spread the rumour."

"I wonder you did not take the knife from her," observed Ellis.

"If I had she would only have used a smaller knife. Well," continued Miss Gordon, "on that fatal night Laura was particularly angry with Edgar because she had been informed by Rudolph that he was flirting with Polly Horley. However, I managed to soothe her, and, as Rudolph never came for me as he promised, I left this house for the station a few minutes after eleven. When I got near the station I found that I had forgotten my purse and returned for it; then, Dr. Ellis," said Janet, clasping her hands, "I came on a terrible sight. Edgar was lying dead on the path, and Laura was lying beside him. The moon showed at intervals, so I saw all quite plainly. Finding Edgar was dead I thought Laura had murdered him, especially as the carving-knife lay on the path beside her. Laura revived very soon, and said she had not killed Edgar. I dragged her into the house; but picking up the carving-knife she said it was the cause of all, and threw it behind some laurels. I had no time to look for it, as my sole object was to get Laura away. I made her put on my hat and cloak and take my purse, telling her to go to Mrs. Amber's and remain in her bedroom, and that I would impersonate her and see the matter through. Laura was beside herself with terror, saying that she was innocent; but she had wit enough to see her danger if she stayed. Therefore, she braced herself up and went away to take a cab to Pimlico. She got one and arrived at Geneva Square safely."

"Yes, and remained in her bedroom as you told her. Mrs. Amber informed me of that. And you, Miss Gordon?"

"I," said Janet, simply, "assumed my sister's character and ran round to call you to see the corpse. You know the rest."

CHAPTER XVIII
WHAT REALLY HAPPENED

After Janet had finished her history there ensued a short silence. Ellis was lost in admiration at the wonderful pluck and resolution of the girl, which had enabled her to face and carry through a difficult matter for the sake of her weaker sister. Now that the worst was over--since she had rescued Laura Moxton from the ordeal of a public accusation--Janet seemed to be in danger of breaking down. After the tension of nerve and will came the inevitable relaxation. The impulse of Ellis was to take her in his arms, and comfort her with assurances of love and protection. But the time was not yet ripe for him to speak of his personal feelings. There was much to do, much to be learnt, before the crooked could be made straight; therefore Ellis, sacrificing self, began to question Janet on points which did not seem quite clear to him. At his first remark she braced herself and gave him immediate attention.

"If you thought that your sister had killed Moxton, why did you not hide the carving-knife?"

"How could I? She threw it away before I could stop her, and there was no time for me to search. When I sent Laura off, I had to call in you and the police, so I could not go out to look for it in the darkness. Next morning, when I could evade the policeman in charge, I slipped out to search. But by that time the knife was gone."

"Busham took it," said Ellis, with a nod. "I wonder how he found it. There was no need for him to search. It looks as though he knew beforehand that with such a weapon Moxton had been stabbed, and came here to secure it."

Janet mused. "I have my doubts of Mr. Busham," she said at last. "He knows more about the matter than he says. Indeed, I should not be at all surprised to hear that he is the guilty person!"

"Impossible! He declares that he can prove an *alibi*--that at the time of the crime he was talking to a policeman, and afterwards followed your sister to Pimlico."

"Have you seen the policeman?"

"No, but I intend to see him as soon as I learn his name or number from Busham."

"He won't tell it to you."

"I can but try, at all events. To do away with my suspicions he may speak out. But, Miss Gordon, I have yet to learn how Edgar Moxton was killed."

"Laura can tell you that," said Janet, rising. "Now that you have heard my story you must listen to what she has to say; then, doctor, you will see how to save her. I was forced into the position I took up."

"I shall be glad to hear Mrs. Moxton's story. Shall I come with you?"

"No, Laura is not so ill as all that; she is merely lying down in the next room and I will bring her in shortly."

She left Ellis alone for a few minutes, which he employed in considering the possibility of Busham being implicated in the crime--indeed, he himself might be the actual criminal. Zirknitz had seen him following Moxton from the Dukesfield Station, and his subsequent acts were related by himself as harmless; but the story of the conversation with the policeman and the following of Mrs. Moxton to Pimlico might be invented to hide the truth. There was nothing to show that Busham had not murdered Edgar, for at that time he was ignorant that Moxton's will was in existence, and by getting rid of his cousin he might hope to clutch a portion of his uncle's money. Ellis made up his mind to do two things--first to see Busham and learn with whom he had been engaged at the time of the crime; second, to interview the policeman hinted at, and discover if Busham was speaking the truth. While he was arguing the necessity of this course in his own mind, Janet returned with Mrs. Moxton leaning on her arm.

The resemblance between the sisters was striking. They were of the same height, their figures were moulded to the same contour, and in face, feature and colouring they were remarkably alike. The difference between them lay in the expression, and in the character of the eye. Laura's glance was soft and wandering, that of Janet steady and calm; the face of Mrs. Moxton was weak, the countenance of Miss Gordon firm. Janet, indeed, seemed to be the masculine counterpart of her sister; she had all the strength of will and resolution of purpose which the other lacked. She was a being of flesh and blood, Laura a shadow, a feather blown by the wind. At the first sight of her face Ellis no longer wondered that she had married a brute like Moxton. She would have married any man had the necessary force of will been exerted. When Ellis beheld this frail creature, when he recalled the evil, scampish nature of Rudolph Zirknitz, he admired Janet more than ever for the wonderful manner in which she had controlled the pair. She was a female Prospero, who ruled at once a weakly, flighty Ariel and a refined Caliban. It must be admitted, however, that the latter part of the above illustration is too severe on Zirknitz, as he was rather a Lazun, a Duc de Richelieu, a Count D'Orsay than the son of Sycorax. However, he was certainly a scamp and dangerous.

Mrs. Moxton, who looked ill and weary, bowed in silence to Ellis, and sank exhausted into the chair vacated by her sister. Janet took a seat beside her and motioned with her head that the doctor should do the same. Ellis obeyed and looked at Mrs. Moxton with some curiosity, but more eagerness, for from her lips he hoped to learn sufficient to indicate the mysterious assassin of Moxton. But the widow, with her eyes fixed on the fire, seemed in no hurry to begin.

"Laura, dear," said Janet, in a coaxing tone, such as a nurse would use to a fractious child, "this is our best friend, Dr. Ellis. He is the only one who can help us out of our difficulties, and I want you to tell him all you remember about Edgar's death."

Mrs. Moxton uttered a low wail, and with a shudder covered her face. When she did speak, it was in so low a tone that Ellis could with difficulty catch what she was saying. "Shall I ever forget that horrible night?" she murmured.

"Tell Dr. Ellis about it, dear," urged Janet, and after a pause Mrs. Moxton did as she was requested. At first her voice was low and nervous, but as she proceeded in the recital it grew powerful. Her nerves responded to the demand made upon them, and gave her a surprising strength of speech in comparison with her frail body. From a physiological standpoint, Ellis was as much interested in her as in the story she told.

"Edgar and I quarrelled on that night about Polly Horley," she began, "for Rudolph told me that he was paying attention to that horrid woman. Edgar swore that it was not true, and I wanted to go to the music-hall to see for myself. He refused to take me and flung out of doors in a great rage. Then Janet came, and her company and conversation calmed me. When she went, and I was left alone, I grew frightened, and got out the carving-knife. I heard Edgar come in at the gate and, not thinking, I ran to open the door with the knife in my hand. When I met him he was on the step, but seeing the knife, and knowing how furious I could be, I suppose he grew frightened. At any rate, he ran back to the gate. I followed, calling out: 'Edgar, Edgar, what is the matter?' When I came up to him he must have thought I meant to strike him, for he was half drunk at the time. His face was white and terrified as I saw in the moonlight; although, as the night was cloudy, that was not very strong."

"I remember the night," interpolated Ellis, "it was windy and rainy, with a fitful moonlight showing through the flying clouds. Well, Mrs. Moxton, what did your husband do when you came up to him?"

"He seized me by the throat," said the widow, hysterically. "I believe that, being half intoxicated, he wished to kill me, and I struggled to get away. But he held me tightly, so that I could not cry out. We were pressed right against the gate. I held the knife above my head, as I was afraid of hurting him with it."

"Why did you not drop it?" asked Ellis.

"I don't know. I never thought of dropping it. The more Edgar fought with me the tighter I held it. He was strangling me, and I could not cry out. Then I saw, all at once, a man on the other side of the gate."

"Could you describe his looks?" asked Ellis, eagerly.

Mrs. Moxton shook her head. "Remember it was a darkish night, with only occasional gleams of moonlight. I was struggling with Edgar, and, holding me by the throat, he had half strangled me. As I said, I held up the knife out of the way. The man on the other side of the gate wore a tall hat and a great coat with a fur collar. I tried to call out to Edgar, but he did not see the man. Suddenly the stranger snatched the knife out of my hand, and struck at Edgar's back. Edgar gave a yell which, I wonder, was not heard all over Dukesfield, so loud it was. He fell forward on me, and crushed by his weight, worn with the struggle, and terrified by the murder, I fainted clean away. The last thing I remember was that Edgar lay over me, struggling and moaning."

"Was the man still at the gate after he struck the blow?"

"I don't know. When I came to myself Janet was bending over me, and I was so frightened that I could explain nothing. After that I picked up the knife which was lying by Edgar's body and flung it over some bushes against the fence. Then Janet hurried me away, and told me she would take my place and deny everything. I was so dazed that I did not know what I was doing. I ran down to the cab-rank and told a cabman to drive me to Pimlico. He did so, and I recovered myself sufficiently in the cab to pay him, and to slip into the house with the latchkey which Janet had pushed into my hand. I knew that she still had our old room, so I ran up to it without seeing anyone, and locked myself in."

"Mrs. Amber told me that you isolated yourself for weeks."

"I did so by Janet's advice, lest Mrs. Amber should recognise me. Janet came to see me a few days afterwards, and told me about the inquest."

"Did you call at Geneva Square?" asked Ellis, turning to Miss Gordon. "That is strange, for Mrs. Amber particularly explained that until a few days ago no one called save Schwartz."

"I paid a visit one night when Mrs. Amber was at the theatre," explained Janet, "and I bribed Sarah, the servant--a most venal creature--to say nothing about it. It was necessary that I should tell Laura what had taken place, and hear her story. Now you know, doctor, why I fenced with you and refused to tell the truth. I was afraid lest my sister should be brought into the matter."

"But Mrs. Moxton is innocent, and you knew it," protested Ellis.

"Yes, I am innocent," wailed Mrs. Moxton, "but what could I do in the face of all I have told you. I cannot hold my tongue like Janet, or foresee things as she does. In one way or another I should have betrayed myself and perhaps have been arrested. Janet was right, Janet was wise to advise me to stay at Pimlico. I feigned ill-health, and would not let Mrs. Amber into my room lest she should get to know too much. Only Sarah knew me, as I had to confide in her to get food. But she held her tongue."

"She nearly betrayed you though, Mrs. Moxton, by taking those cuffs to Mrs. Amber."

"That was a mistake," said the widow. "In touching Edgar's body I got blood on my cuffs, and threw them aside in the bedroom. I never thought of hiding them, and Sarah took them downstairs without consulting me."

"How did you manage to keep up the concealment of your identity to the end?"

"I managed that," said Janet, in her firm, clear voice. "I called when I knew that Mrs. Amber was absent, and told Laura that, on account of Busham, I intended to take her away. When Mrs. Amber came back, of course, she thought that I had been in my bedroom all the time, and that Laura had called for me. She was so deceived," added Janet, smiling, "that she told me how ill I looked after lying so long in bed. But I am afraid I did look ill, with all the worry."

"I don't wonder at it," said Ellis, sympathetically. "I cannot imagine how you have borne up through all the troubles you have had. Few women would have taken another's burden so bravely on their shoulders as you have done, Miss Gordon."

"Indeed, she has been the best of sisters," exclaimed Mrs. Moxton, with tears in her eyes. "Never shall I forget what Janet has done for me."

"At some cost to yourself, dear Laura," said Janet, patting her sister's hand. "After all, my defence of you has cost you your fortune."

"I don't mind in the least, Janet. Let Mr. Busham take all so long as he holds his tongue."

"I fancy Busham will keep silent for his own sake," remarked Ellis, drily, "for I feel certain that he has more to do with this murder than you think."

"You don't believe that he killed Edgar?"

"I might even go so far as that, but I must collect sufficient evidence to justify such belief. However, we can talk of that later. With reference to the destruction of the will, Miss Gordon, you need not worry about that."

"Oh, but I do. Laura will lose her father-in-law's money."

"Not by the destruction of the will, because the original document is in my possession, and what Busham burnt was a copy carefully prepared by myself and my friend Mr. Cass."

CHAPTER XIX
THE RED POCKET-BOOK

"Do you mean to say that the paper Mr. Busham destroyed was not Edgar's will?" asked Janet, while her sister uttered an exclamation of joy.

"I do mean it. I reported your conversation about our mutual friend to Cass, and we both agreed that he was not to be trusted with the original will. Cass, who is clever at imitating handwriting, procured a sheet of paper similar, to that upon which the will was written, and copied it out, signatures and all. I am afraid it was a species of forgery, but as it had to be done if we wished to checkmate Busham, we contrived the crime. It was just as well we did so, Miss Gordon, as Busham had no compunction in destroying the will. My wonder is that a clever pettifogger such as he is could not see that the document was forged. Singular obtuseness on his part."

"If it had remained longer in his possession, he no doubt would have discovered the truth," replied Janet, "but, if you remember, he merely glanced at it, and not crediting me with so clever an idea as substituting a copy for the original, took it for the genuine will. I can never thank you sufficiently, doctor, for what you have done."

"Nor I either," chimed in Laura, who, seeing that there was a prospect of recovering her husband's money, plucked up her spirits. "Now Mr. Busham will not be able to rob me."

"H'm!" said Janet, with a frown, "putting the will out of the question, my dear, you are still in the same dangerous position as formerly. If he finds out the trick Dr. Ellis has played him, he may denounce you."

"He will do so at his own risk," cried Ellis, promptly. "And you may be sure he will never learn the truth from me until it can be told with safety to Mrs. Moxton. Leave Busham to me. I shall know how to deal with him. In some way or another we must clear up this mystery, and exonerate Mrs. Moxton. If there was only some clue."

Janet and Laura looked meaningly at one another. "There *is* a clue, although it is only a slight one," said Miss Gordon, hesitatingly.

"To the identity of the murderer?"

"No, but a clue which may lead to his discovery. When Laura was lying in a faint, the man who stabbed Edgar robbed him of his pocket-book."

"But how could he do that without Moxton recognising him?" asked Ellis. "You know that Moxton did not die at once, but lived long enough to scrawl those blood signs on his arm denouncing Zirknitz. Now, I know that your brother is innocent, as he has established an *alibi* with the assistance of his landlady, Mrs. Pastor."

"I cannot explain that, doctor, but undoubtedly Edgar thought that Rudolph stabbed him, and so wrote on his arm to let Laura know."

"You can read the cryptogram, I presume, Mrs. Moxton?"

"Oh, yes, I know the signs very well. Janet taught them to me, and I showed them to Edgar for amusement. He, no doubt, wished me to know that Rudolph had stabbed him, but why he used the signs I cannot say. He hated Rudolph always, and would have got him into trouble if he could."

"Well," said Ellis, after a pause, "I can conceive no reason why he acted as he did. I don't suppose the truth will ever be revealed. But about this pocket-book, Mrs. Moxton. How do you know that the murderer took it?"

"I only think so. It was a red Morocco pocket-book with Edgar's initials on it in gold. He had it when he went out that night, and I saw him put it into his breast pocket. When Janet came to Pimlico I asked her if she had seen it, as I thought that there might be some bank-notes in it, and we needed money badly."

"Did he carry money in it?"

"Yes, when he had any."

"On that night were there any notes in the pocket-book?"

"I cannot say. Rudolph declares that he won twenty pounds from Edgar on that night. Edgar could not pay him save with an I.O.U., so I don't think there could have been money in the book."

"Then why should the assassin steal it?"

"Why, indeed!" echoed Janet, who had been silent for some time; "that is what we wish to find out. As Edgar's jewellery was untouched, robbery could not have been the motive of the crime. I believe myself that the pocket-book must have contained some papers of value to the murderer. No person but he could have taken it, for I examined very carefully the clothes Edgar wore when he was killed, and could not find the pocket-book. Dr. Ellis," said Janet, earnestly, "it seems to me that if you can find that book, you will be able to lay hands on the criminal."

"Possibly, Miss Gordon. But in what direction am I to look. In the autumn many men wear fur-lined overcoats, so that is not a strong clue. Moreover, the pocket-book must long since have been destroyed if the murderer valued his neck. No; on the whole I think it will be best to see Busham, as I said before. My movements will depend upon the sort of information he supplies."

"He will tell you nothing."

"Not of his own free will, perhaps, but I maybe in a position to force his confidence."

It was now late, as this conversation between the three had lasted a considerable time. Laura looked so fatigued and ill that Ellis, in his capacity of medical man, insisted that she should retire. "Take as much rest and sleep as you can, Mrs. Moxton, and don't worry. I will help you all I can in this matter, and I have no doubt I shall be able to clear you of all suspicion. Good-night."

Ellis was accompanied to the door by Janet, who was hopeful of his success.

"You will be certain to solve this mystery--you and Mr. Cass," said she. "Think how much you have discovered already by observation."

"And if I do solve it, and right your sister, what then, Miss Gordon?"

Janet laughed, and, in the kindly darkness, blushed. "We can talk of that when the time comes," she said, answering his thought after the manner of women.

With this assurance the doctor was fain to be content, and departed without gaining the kiss of which he had dreamt. Needless to say, he was more in love than ever, and thanked Heaven that he had been brought into contact with so noble and earnest a woman as Janet Gordon. Anxious to hear the result of his friend's visit, Cass was waiting up for him, and into his astonished ears Ellis poured the whole story which exonerated and cleansed Janet. Cass admitted that he had been wrong in his estimate of her character.

"But how was one to read it properly under the circumstances," he said testily. "I could not believe in the woman without proof."

"I did," said Ellis, smiling.

"Because you are in love; yours was not legitimate belief. On the same mad principle you would have trusted Lucrezia Borgia. Still, your experience is sufficiently strange, and I am glad that your instinct has been justified. Miss Gordon, on the face of it, has proved herself a singularly able, and, I may say, a noble woman; but I must see more of her, and learn to know her better before I can rescind my former opinion--that she is not the wife for you."

"To know her is to love her," said Ellis, with deep emotion.

"Ah, you see I don't know her, therefore I cannot love her; if I did you might object. However, the main question at present is how to extricate her and Mrs. Moxton from their equivocal position. Until the assassin is found, and all is made plain, Mrs. Moxton dare not explain our trick to Busham or claim her property. If she did he might be dangerous."

"Can he be dangerous?"

"So far as inclination goes I should say so, but whether he has the power is another question, and one not so easily answered. However, for your satisfaction, Bob, I can tell you that Busham is a liar. While you were at Myrtle Villa I went round to Drake at the Police Office and tried to find out if Busham had spoken to any policeman on that night. If you remember he declared that he held a long conversation with one at, or near, the station. He trusts to that for an *alibi*."

"But Drake does not know Busham; he could tell you nothing, Harry."

"Quite so, but he could tell me who was on duty on that night. I did not inform him of my reasons, save that I was curious on my own account to learn who killed Moxton, so I found out the names of the police on duty that night. Queerly enough their term of service has come round again for night duty, so I went out and questioned at least half a dozen about Busham."

"Well?" asked Ellis, impatiently.

"Well, Busham is a liar; he spoke to none of them, and none spoke to him. They never saw a gentleman of his description about on that night, so I judged that he dodged after Moxton in the shadows to avoid recognition. Now, Bob, your best plan is to see Busham and accuse him; then we shall see if he can bring forward in his defence this supposititious policeman."

"Good. I'll call on our mutual friend to-morrow. But I shall see Zirknitz first."

"What for?"

"To ask him how Busham was dressed on that night. As the police would not recognise Busham by his face, they might by his dress. In that way we can learn if anyone of them saw him following Moxton after they left the railway station."

Having decided upon this course, which, under the circumstances, was the most sensible, both men retired to bed. Next morning, after a further discussion with Cass, the doctor set out for Bloomsbury. As yet he had not many patients, so he could afford the time, but his practice was increasing, and he foresaw that unless he could bring the matter of the murder to a speedy conclusion, he would be obliged to throw it over altogether. But on Janet's account he was unwilling to do this.

As usual, M. Zirknitz was still in bed, and Ellis waited for some time in the gorgeous sitting-room, which its owner--apparently--had created out of nothing. When the Austrian made his appearance he was as lively as ever, and greeted Ellis in his most genial manner.

"Ah, Ellis, *mon ami, mon cher*, so you have arrived once more. Is it to take me to a prison or to join me at *déjeuner*--the latter, I hope; friendship is so much more charming than enmity."

"I have come only to ask you a few questions, Zirknitz; also to tell you something which may astonish you."

"Astonish me! *C'est une mauvaise plaisanterie, mon cher*. I am never astonished at anything in this best of all possible worlds. You have not read *Candide*, in which that saying occurs? No. Ah, you should. Voltaire is the most witty of his race. *Eh bien!* What is your astonishing news?"

"I know your history and that of your sisters, and I have learnt how Miss Gordon took the place of Mrs. Moxton to fight her battles."

"You know that? Ah, well, Janet must have told you. If she did, she is right. Janet can do no wrong. She is the dearest and most excellent sister in the world."

"Are you the best brother to her?"

"I? *Mon, ami*, I am a scamp. I have no good in me. If I had it would not be so creditable to Janet that she is fond of me. So she has told you all her intrigues. What can I do?"

"Inform me about Busham. You saw him on that night?"

"*Oui da!* He followed that poor Edgar from the station."

"How was he dressed?"

Zirknitz reflected. "It was cold that night," said he, musingly. "I put on a fur coat. Eh! Ah, yes. Busham had a coat of the same and a tall hat. I can say no more than that."

A fur-lined coat, a tall hat. This was precisely the scanty description given by Laura of her momentary glimpse of the assassin. What if the lawyer, after all, should be the guilty person? Full of excitement Ellis detailed to Zirknitz his suspicions, and cited the fact of the red pocket-book. The Austrian uttered an exclamation of astonishment on hearing that this was missing.

"Edgar, excellent Edgar, had it in his pocket at the music-hall. Eh! yes, I quite remember. He took out the book to show me a bill."

"A bill? What kind of a bill?"

"A bill of exchange or a promissory note. Now you speak, *mon cher ami*, it all comes back to me. Edgar showed me the name of his father on the bill and declared that it was forged."

"A forged bill!" said Ellis, "and in the pocket-book which was stolen? Ah, this, then, may be the motive for the crime. Zirknitz, did Moxton say who had forged the bill?"

"Eh? No. He said, 'My Rudolph, see what I got from Busham this night.'"

"Busham! Busham! Could he have forged the bill?"

"Eh? No, I think not, or he would not give it to Edgar."

"Still, a forged bill, obtained from Busham, and he followed Edgar out of the station. He wore a tall hat and a fur coat. As the assassin was dressed the same it might be--By Heavens! Zirknitz, I believe that Busham is the guilty person, after all."

Zirknitz shrugged his shoulders, but did not offer an opinion, and as the doctor did not think that there was anything further to be learnt from him, he rose to go. At the door, however, he paused, and made a chance remark which gained him greater results than any of his previous questions.

"I forgot to tell you," said Ellis, "that I have tricked Busham. He thinks that he has a claim to a portion of Mrs. Moxton's property because he destroyed the will. But what he destroyed, M. Zirknitz, was a copy made by me; the original is in my possession."

Rudolph's eyes sparkled. "Then Laura will inherit all Moxton's wealth?"

"Undoubtedly, as soon as she can claim it, without risking any danger from Busham. He knows too much."

"But not as much as I know. Listen, *mon ami*. I can tell you a great deal about Busham which will help you to save Laura. Eh, yes, I will see that she gets the money of that poor Edgar."

"So that you may get a share of it, I suppose?" said Ellis, drily. Zirknitz laughed and shrugged his shoulders. "But, certainly-- Why not? I am her brother; I need money. If I help her, she must help me. Listen! *mon cher.*"

With this exordium Zirknitz poured forth into Ellis's ears a story about the lawyer and about his own treachery which at once pleased and horrified Ellis. He did not know whether most to hate or admire the scamp; but in the end he decided that it would be diplomatic to hide his feelings, and so ended his visit.

CHAPTER XX
BUSHAM AT BAY

It was in a state of subdued excitement that Ellis left the rooms of Zirknitz. He now seemed to be nearer solving the mystery than he had ever been before. There was no doubt that Moxton had been murdered in order to obtain the forged bill; but Ellis was uncertain in his own mind whether Busham had actually struck the blow. A silk hat and a fur-lined coat was not a distinctive dress on a cold evening for any man--a dozen might wear it. Still, the coincidence of dress was striking. Busham might be the criminal, after all, and Ellis drove directly to Esher Lane for the purpose of satisfying himself on this point.

What the doctor particularly wished to know was who had forged the elder Moxton's name? If Busham had done so he would scarcely have given the bill to Edgar, who had no great love for him. To hand him over an incriminating document and then murder him to get it back again would have been the height of folly. If, therefore, Busham was innocent of the forgery, he would scarcely risk his life in endeavouring to recover the bill. Thus, if anyone had a reason to desire the death of Edgar, it must have been the forger himself. Having committed one crime he certainly would not hesitate to commit a second, if only to conceal the first. This theory was excellent, and Ellis wished to prove its truth. To do so, it was necessary that he should learn the name of the man who had forged the bill. Busham had given the document to Edgar Moxton, as was asserted by Zirknitz, therefore Busham could inform him of what he wished to know. But would he do so? Ellis, for want of experience of the man, could not answer this question, and arrived at Esher Lane in a state of perplexity. However, his head was clear and his will determined--a most necessary frame of mind for anyone who had to deal with so crafty a creature as Busham.

The office was as dingy and dirty as ever. The lean clerks still scribbled interminable folios, and strained their eyes in the uncertain light. From the inner room came the rasping cough of Busham, which showed that he was alive and plotting. Ellis sent in his card, which was received by the lawyer with anything but pleasure. However, he did not think it wise to betray any fear of his visitor, so gave orders that he was to be admitted at once. More than that, he threw into his greeting as much cordiality as was possible with one of his detestable nature.

"I am glad to see you, doctor," said he, pointing to one of the two chairs. "That seems strange, does it not? We had a tiff last time we met here, eh? Quite so. But I never bear malice, not I. How is Mrs. Moxton?"

"The true Mrs. Moxton is quite well."

Busham's naturally pale face became of a greenish hue. "What do you mean with your 'true Mrs. Moxton?'" he demanded, narrowing his eyes until they looked like those of a cat.

"What I say, and what you know. Janet Gordon, to fight her sister's battles, took that sister's place."

"You are well informed," sneered Busham. "On whose authority?"

"I have the best authority. Miss Gordon told me herself."

"How dare you say that I knew of this plot!" cried the lawyer, savagely. "Ridiculous! I know nothing about the sisters."

"That is a lie!" replied Ellis, coolly. "You know everything about them. For months you have been watching for an opportunity to get them into your toils."

"Who says this?"

"Rudolph Zirknitz."

"Bah! that silly fool! What does he know?"

"More than you think," retorted Ellis. "Zirknitz is a scamp, but no fool, and he told me all about the questions you had asked him. He even mentioned the sums of money you have paid him for his information."

"What information?" said Busham, fighting every inch.

"Is it necessary for me to inform you?" questioned Ellis, with icy contempt.

"What information?" repeated the lawyer.

"He told you that the supposed Mrs. Moxton was really Janet Gordon. He betrayed his sisters for money like the contemptible creature he is, and in turn he has betrayed you."

"I don't understand your hint of betrayal."

"I think you do. But if you wish me to be more explicit, I can inform you that Zirknitz saw you following Moxton on that night."

Busham sneered, and his brow cleared. "So you said when Mrs. Moxton--I beg your pardon--Miss Gordon was here. I then admitted that I was at Dukesfield on that night, and gave my reasons for being there. Also, I gave an account of my actions."

"I know you did, Mr. Busham. A very pretty account which did justice to your imagination."

"I told the truth," cried Busham, gnawing his lip.

"No, you did not. You told what suited your purpose. You spoke to no policeman on that night, for those who were on duty then have all been closely questioned. You never followed Mrs. Moxton to Pimlico, but you called there later and bribed the servant, Sarah, to tell you the truth."

"Who says I did?"

"Zirknitz. I am afraid you were a trifle overconfident of his silence, Mr. Busham."

"Zirknitz is a liar!"

"Oh, no, only a traitor who changes sides when he sees a chance of making money."

"He won't make any out of his sisters," growled Busham. "I have burnt that will, and the Moxton property will come to me."

Ellis smiled when he thought on how slight a foundation this belief rested. "Well, we will say nothing about the will But even though you have destroyed it, Mrs. Moxton takes a great portion of her husband's property as his widow."

"She sha'n't have one penny," snarled Busham. "A jade, an adventuress and a murderess! that's what she is. If she refuses to give me the whole of the Moxton property, I'll denounce her. He! he! then she will be hanged."

"I doubt it, Busham. There is a prejudice against hanging women in this country. As to your saying that she killed Moxton, that is a lie, and you know it. The man who murdered your cousin wore a silk hat and fur coat."

"Who says so?"

"Mrs. Moxton herself. She saw the man strike the blow, but could not recognise him."

"Oh, that is an invention to save her neck," scoffed Busham. "A man in a silk hat and a fur coat? Bosh! Who is the man!"

"Well, I am not quite clear on that point," replied Ellis, speaking very slowly, "but I fancied he might be you."

Busham started from his seat with a kind of screech hardly human. "I?" he gasped. "You dare to accuse me of that crime! And on what grounds?"

"You wore a similar dress on the night you followed Moxton."

"Who says I did?"

"Your dear friend, M. Zirknitz."

Busham ground his teeth, and said something not precisely complimentary to the Austrian. After a time he recovered his calmness, but not his colour. "You accuse me of murdering Moxton?" he said.

"Oh, no, I don't accuse you, I merely state that such might be the case."

"Bah! The accusation is not worth considering. What motive could I have for killing my cousin! It is true that his father altered his will at the last moment and left everything to Edgar. What then? I had sufficient influence with him to finger that money, and I certainly intended to do so. Why should I risk my neck to upset all my plans?"

"You might have hoped to get the money after Moxton's death, or, at least, a share of it."

"Don't deceive yourself," snapped the lawyer. "I hoped for none of it. Edgar told me that, after his marriage, he had made a will leaving all to his wife. What motive, then, had I to commit so purposeless a crime. I could manage Edgar because I knew him; but I never met,--I never saw Mrs. Moxton, and could hope to gain no influence over her, especially with that infernal sister in the way. If she--"

"Speak more respectfully of Miss Gordon," interrupted the doctor, angrily. "She is my friend, and I will not permit a word against her. You say that Mrs. Moxton killed her husband. Prove it!"

"She was always quarrelling with him," replied Busham, sullenly. "I know that for a fact, because Edgar told me so. He said that he was afraid of his wife, that she frequently threatened him with the carving-knife. When I heard of the murder next morning I went down to see Mrs. Moxton, as I was certain she had killed Edgar. As I walked up the garden I saw the flash of steel in a laurel bush, and on going to it I found a knife stuck in one of the branches. It was a carving-knife, and there was blood on the blade and the handle. I was certain then that Mrs. Moxton was guilty, but having my own ends to gain I did not denounce her then, but simply slipped the knife up my sleeve and went away. I produced it as you saw to make Miss Gordon--for thanks to Zirknitz I knew my visitor was not Mrs. Moxton--give up the will. She made the exchange and took away the knife. I burnt the will as you saw, and by destroying it could hope to get a portion of the property. Now I mean to have the whole, or else I shall denounce Mrs. Moxton."

"I don't think you'll do that, Busham, for I shall then state that you committed a felony by burning the will. No, no, whatever happens you can't afford to denounce Mrs. Moxton. You might frighten her, and, perhaps--as she is only a woman--Miss Gordon, but you can't frighten me. As to your finding of the knife, Mrs. Moxton threw it into the laurel bush after the murder, but she did not use it."

"You will find it difficult to prove that," snarled Busham, beginning to feel beaten. "If she did not use it, who did?"

"The man in the fur coat, who snatched it from her when she was in her husband's grip."

"And who is the man in the fur coat?"

"I think you know, Busham."

"Indeed, I don't, confound you!"

"At least you know the name of the man who endorsed that bill."

With a gasp the lawyer started out of his chair. "Bill? What bill?"

"The forged bill which you gave to Moxton at the Merryman Music-Hail on the night of the murder."

"I gave no bill. I know of none."

"Oh, yes, you do. Moxton showed the bill to Zirknitz and told him that it was forged on his father. It was placed in a red pocket-book, Mr. Busham, and that pocket-book was stolen from the corpse."

"Lies! Lies! All lies!" raved Busham, stamping. "I know nothing of any bill! I don't know who killed Moxton!"

Ellis did not waste words, but rising to his feet glanced at his watch with a calm air. "I must go now," said he. "I shall give you five days to tell the truth, Mr. Busham. Failing that, I shall place the whole matter in the hands of the police, and re-open the case. Good-day, sir;" and with that last warning Ellis walked out of the room.

With a white face and a haggard expression, Busham sat for an hour or more in his chair. Twice one of his clerks opened the door and looked in, but awed by the expression of terror in the lawyer's eyes, withdrew. At last Busham wiped his brow, which was beaded with perspiration, and rose to his feet. "Shall I fly or stay?" he asked himself; then, bringing down his fist on the table, he cried: "No, by Heaven! I'll stay and fight it out!"

CHAPTER XXI
THE BLIND GIRL

In compliment to the great poet of his nation, Herr Schwartz dignified his English home with the name of Goethe Cottage. It was a one-storeyed house of no great size, built somewhat in the style of a bungalow, and standing in a fairly large garden, at the bottom of a rural *cul-de-sac*, termed Alma Road. Shortly after his visit to the lawyer, Dr. Ellis called at this place, and having advised Schwartz of his coming, found the German and Captain Garret awaiting his arrival. So eager were they to welcome him that they appeared at the gate before the bell ceased to jingle.

"Mine goot doctor," cried Schwartz, beaming, with outstretched hands, "you haf gome at last to zee boor liddle Hilda!"

"Glad to see you, Dr. Ellis," said Garret, jerking out his words in abrupt military style. "We have long expected your visit. Come in."

The three walked towards the house through a theatrical-looking garden, with many coloured glass balls ranged on squat pedestals along the borders of the flower-beds. There was also a tiny fountain, in which a small Triton spouted a smaller stream of water out of a conch-shell, an arbour fiery red with Virginia creeper, and wide walks of white pebbles, which threw back a glare, even under the pale rays of the late autumn sun. The house was surrounded by a wide verandah with gaily-striped red and white sun-blinds, cane lounging-chairs and marble-topped iron tables. Within, Ellis found the place luxuriously furnished, but also theatrical in taste, and he was shown into a drawing-room where intrusive colours of scarlet and magenta inflicted torture on a sensitive eye. Schwartz had money and a love of comfort; but the complacent way in which he looked round this terrible apartment showed that he was absolutely without the artistic sense. A woman might have softened the general glaring effect of the room; but the only woman in the house was blind, and could have no idea of the crude, ill-matched colouring by which she was surrounded.

When they sat down Ellis looked at his companions, and was astonished how ill Schwartz appeared to be. Garret, as formerly, was haggard, lean and gentlemanly, with the same military bearing and bored expression.

Evidently he was a man who had, as the saying is, "gone the pace," and now, in his middle age--he was between forty and fifty--lacked vitality and zest. As usual he was carefully dressed, and looked eminently well-bred and well-groomed beside his patron and friend. Schwartz himself was less complacent and jolly, also he was lean in comparison with his former portly figure, and his clothes hung loosely on his limbs. Instead of his face being smooth and red, it was now pallid, and wrinkled, and although he attempted to be his usual happy self, the attempt was an obvious effort. Occasionally he stole a troubled glance at the Captain, but that gentleman hardly looked at him and manifested supreme indifference. Only when the conversation had to do with Hilda did he wake up and take any interest in what was going on.

"You are not looking well yourself, Herr Schwartz," said Ellis, when the trio were seated and refreshments had been produced by the hospitable German.

"Ach! I am ferry vell," replied Schwartz, hastily. "The hot dimes of the zun haf made me thin, and I haf moch thinking apout the liddle Hilda."

"Oh, you must keep up your spirits about that. I may be able to restore her sight. Was she born blind?"

"No," interposed Garret. "Took notice like other children for a few weeks, but afterwards the sight went. Do you think you can cure her?"

"I must make an examination first. It is impossible for me to give an opinion before then."

"Das is right, doctor. You vill zee the liddle Hilda at vonce. I would gif all my moneys if you could make her zee."

"You are very fond of her, Herr Schwartz?"

Tears came into the German's eyes, for after the manner of his nation he was emotional and sentimental and easily touched. "The liddle Hilda is the light of mine life," he said, in tones of deep feeling. "I haf lofed her for years, and she is to me mine own child. I am her zecond vater."

"Father and mother and everything else," jerked Garret. "Much better than a scamp like me."

"No, no," protested Schwartz, but with a ring of insincerity in his voice, which Ellis at once detected. "You are a goot man, mein frind."

"Can I see Miss Garret now?"

"Dis ferry moment," cried the German, getting up in a violent hurry. "Will you gome with me, doctor? And you, Garret?"

"I shall stay here, Schwartz. Better have as few in the room as possible, or Hilda will be nervous."

"Ach! is dat zo? Then I vill not sday. Gome, doctor." The room at the back of the house, into which Schwartz introduced Ellis, was like a fairy palace. A large, airy, high-roofed apartment, decked and furnished with rainbow hues. Chinese paper of the willow-plate pattern figured on the walls, curtains blue as a midsummer sky draped the French windows, the carpet was of the same cerulean tint, and the furniture was upholstered in azure and white. Hothouse flowers were placed in every corner, there was a grand piano, and many birds in gilded cages made the room re-echo with tuneful strains. The windows were many and large, admitting ample light, and looking out on to a velvet lawn bounded by a tall hedge of laurel. Ellis had never seen a more pretty or cheerful apartment, and felt sad at the irony which placed amidst all this beauty and light so attractive to the eye a blind girl. She was seated at the piano when they entered, but rose when she heard the door open.

Hilda Garret was tall for her age, in spite of the tender diminutive bestowed on her by Schwartz. Her face was as pale as marble, and as beautiful as that of the Venus de Medici. Indeed, in her white robe, with pallid face and still looks, she was not unlike a statue. The lack of eyesight took away all expression, and she lived and moved in a world of shadows. Ellis was profoundly touched by her beauty and helplessness, and by the tender little cry she uttered when Schwartz took her hand.

"Mine lofely laty, I haf brought Dr. Ellis to zee you. He is mine goot friend, and glever. He vill mak you to zee, mine heart."

"Oh, doctor," said Hilda, clasping her hands, and speaking in a low, but musical voice, "can you give me back my sight?"

"That I cannot say as yet," replied Ellis. "I cannot perform miracles. If your sight can be restored, I hope to restore it. But I must first ask you a few questions and examine your eyes."

"Aha! I vill go away."

"No, no, papa, you must stay. I wish my father would come in also. I want him to hold my hand and give me courage."

"Zo!" replied Schwartz, with a sad expression at this preference. "Vait, mine liddle Hilda, I vill pring your vater to you."

Hilda nodded and a charming smile overspread her pale face. When Schwartz left the room she asked Ellis to let her pass her hand over his face, as she wished to know his looks. Ellis readily consented, and Hilda, with the delicate touch of the blind, ran her fingers over his features. "You are nice-looking," she said naïvely, when this was done. "I like nice-looking people."

"Thank you," answered Ellis, laughing. "I am obliged for the compliment, Miss Garret. And now I must ask you a few questions."

To this Hilda readily consented. It is not necessary to set forth the conversation or examination *in extensor*, as the questions were purely technical.

Captain Garret entered, and held Hilda's hand while Ellis made an examination of her eyes. This took some time, but was unsatisfactory, as Ellis could not bring himself to pronounce an opinion. Privately he thought that he could cure the cataract by an operation; but lacking the self-confidence which a great man should have, he hesitated to express his private views.

"I must make another examination," he said, after an exhaustive conversation, "before I can commit myself to an opinion. Yet I think I can give you some hope."

"Oh, father!" Hilda uttered the words in a thrilling voice, and Ellis glanced at Captain Garret. He did not look pleased; indeed he frowned and withdrew his hand from that of his daughter. It occurred to Ellis that the Captain did not wish Hilda to regain her sight. The expression of anger was only a flash, but Ellis saw it, and gained the above impression. Had Schwartz been in the room, the Captain might have controlled himself better, but Schwartz had not returned after Hilda's cry for her father. Even on his short acquaintance, Ellis could not but think how the good German must have suffered from his voluntary exclusion from his darling. However, Garret said nothing at the moment, and the doctor addressed himself to Hilda.

"I shall come and see you in two or three days," he said. "But you must keep yourself cheerful and not mope. Have you no companion?"

"Schwartz and myself," put in Garret.

"I mean no female companion?"

"Janet Gordon comes to see me sometimes," said Hilda. "I am very fond of her. She is so kind and good. I wish she would come again."

"She shall come again, Miss Garret. I will speak to her myself."

Garret uttered an exclamation. "Do you know her, doctor?"

"Very well. She is staying at Myrtle Villa with her sister, Mrs. Moxton."

"H'm!" said the Captain, with a glance at Hilda. "I don't know if Schwartz will like her to come here again."

"Why not?"

"I will tell you outside, or perhaps Schwartz will tell you himself."

"But I want Janet to come," cried Hilda, piteously. "I love her!"

Again the flash of anger passed over Garret's face, but he only patted her hand softly. "If Schwartz permits her to come, she shall come," he said; "and now, doctor, we had better go."

"I think so. Good-bye, Miss Garret. I may be able to cure you, and if you want Miss Gordon, you shall have her for a companion."

"Thank you, doctor, thank you," and as they left the room Hilda began to play a triumphal march on the piano. The words of Ellis had inspired her with hope and confidence.

Captain Garret immediately addressed the doctor when they left the room. "I could not speak to you plainly, in there," he said abruptly, "but I have the strongest objection to Miss Gordon coming here."

"On account of the murder?"

"Yes. Hilda knows nothing of that, therefore I did not explain. If Miss Gordon is her companion, she may hear of the crime; and think of the shock it would be to her delicate nerves!"

"She will never hear anything of the crime from Miss Gordon. That lady is most discreet."

"She is clever, I don't deny, doctor--too clever, in my opinion. But she is shady. She sold programmes at the Merryman Music-Hall; she is not the kind of companion I should choose for my daughter."

This came well from Captain Garret, who had been cashiered for cheating, who lived on another man's money, and who was an out-and-out adventurer. Ellis felt such a contempt for him that he did not argue the question. "Let us hear what Herr Schwartz has to say," he said.

"Schwartz will be of my opinion," said the Captain, gravely.

But here, it appeared, Garret was wrong. Schwartz listened attentively to the recommendation of Ellis that Miss Gordon should be brought to Goethe Cottage as a companion for Hilda. His face grew a shade paler to the doctor's attentive eye, and he appeared to be uneasy. After a sharp glance at Ellis, he made up his mind and spoke it.

"Miss Corton shall gome!" he declared decisively.

"Schwartz!" said Garret, in a warning tone, whereat the usually placid German flew into a rage.

"I say she shall gome!" he cried, in his deepest tones. "Chanet is a goot girl; she vill not dalk of murders and wickednesses. She is glever!"

Garret muttered something not precisely complimentary to Janet, and turned away. The German looked after him with an anxious expression; but finally turned to Ellis with a look of relief. "Dell Chanet to gome," he said, "but she must zay notings of the murders."

"I'll answer for her there," said Ellis, cheerfully.

"And you can make right the liddle Hilda?"

"I think so; but I can answer you for certain next time I come. I shall bring Miss Gordon with me," and so, in spite of Captain Garret, it was arranged.

CHAPTER XXII
JANET'S DISCOVERY

On leaving Goethe Cottage, Ellis jumped on his bicycle, and was soon spinning along the country roads which connected rural Parkmere with the more urban suburb of Dukesfield. Usually Ellis enjoyed the exhilaration of riding and the pleasure of admiring the scenery; but on this occasion, beyond the necessary guidance of his machine, he was preoccupied. It seemed strange to him that Garret should so strongly object to Janet as a companion for his daughter. The Captain was a supremely selfish man, as selfish in every way as Zirknitz, and more vicious. He was indifferent to his daughter, save that he looked upon her as a necessary link to bind him to Schwartz. Schwartz was clever and generous, and devoted to Hilda; he had plenty of money, and Garret, the idle and dissipated, could not do without him. For the furtherance of his plans, he usually let Schwartz manage Hilda, and Hilda's business, as he pleased. It was, therefore, surprising that he should have taken so unusual a step as to object to Miss Gordon.

"Garret and Schwartz can have nothing to do with the murder!" mused Ellis; "they knew Moxton only slightly, and they had no motive to get rid of him. Indeed, his untimely death has lost Schwartz a good customer to his gambling table, if that exists, as is reported; at any-rate, an assiduous attendant at his music-hall. Garret was anxious on Schwartz's account, hence he warned him not to have Janet in the house. He thinks she is too clever; perhaps he fancies she may learn too much. I am too fanciful--too suspicious. Yet Garret certainly mentioned the murder. What is best to be done? Janet must go to Goethe Cottage to keep Hilda cheerful; but shall I tell her of the objections--or this discussion? No, I will not bias her in any way. If there is anything to be found out, she shall discover it herself."

To this wise determination Ellis adhered. On seeing Janet that evening, he merely informed her that Hilda was mopish, and that he wished her to cheer the girl. Janet readily consented to this.

"I am very fond of Hilda," she said earnestly; "and you may be sure I shall do what I can. Does Mr. Schwartz want me to come?"

"Very much. Tell me, Miss Gordon, what is your opinion of him?"

"I think he is a good man, doctor. Several times I have been under the necessity of testing his kindness of heart, and it has never failed me. Then look how good he is to poor Hilda. If she depended upon that selfish father of hers, how wretched she would be."

"Yet she appears to be more attached to her father than to Schwartz."

"I daresay," said Janet, somewhat cynically; "it is that frame of mind which created the proverb about virtue being its own reward. People who do most are thought least of, and it is your selfish person who gets all the love and the praise. Look at my own case. All my life I have put myself aside for Rudolph and Laura; yet they think nothing of me."

"They say they do."

"Mere lip-service!" exclaimed Miss Gordon; "they would not do me a good turn however little trouble it might be. Laura is grateful to me now, because she is yet in danger, and I stand by her; but when all is well, she will think nothing of my services. As for Rudolph, he would borrow my last sixpence, and see me dying of starvation without returning so much as a single penny. Oh, I am under no disillusion about my own folk, doctor! What I do, I do from a sense of duty."

"With regard to your sister I can say nothing, Miss Gordon, as I do not know her sufficiently well; but Zirknitz--well, he is a thoroughly bad lot, and would sell his nearest and dearest at a price."

Janet demurred. "I cannot believe that he is so wicked as that!"

"But he is, and he proved it to me only the other day. He told Busham all about your impersonation of Mrs. Moxton; betrayed all your schemes and plans while you were fighting single-handed against overwhelming odds; and this because Busham paid him. Now, thinking Mrs. Moxton will recover her husband's fortune--for I told him that the real will still existed--he has betrayed all Busham's secret doings to me. What do you think of him now?"

"He is a scoundrel! I will never speak to him again. Oh, doctor, if you only knew what I have done for that man. I knew he was heartless and selfish, but I did not think he was wicked."

"Heartlessness and selfishness usually terminate in wickedness," said Ellis, sententiously. "However, one good result has come out of his evil ways. I have learnt all about Mr. Busham's intrigues, and I have given him a few days to own up."

"That he killed Edgar?" asked Janet, breathlessly.

"No, he did not kill him--at least, I don't think so. But I have insisted upon his revealing the name of the assassin, as I am certain he knows it. In another three days he must tell the truth, or I shall place the matter in the hands of the police."

"Oh! but, Laura; she will be arrested."

"No! I do this to save her from arrest. Busham knows nothing about the false will, because I do not wish to drive him into a corner by telling him how he has been tricked. But he might learn the truth from Zirknitz, to whom it had to be told, that I might learn his true attitude in this matter. If he does learn it he will have Mrs. Moxton arrested. Only by a threat against himself could I keep him in hand."

"What do you think he will do?"

"Ah! that I can't say. I know much, but not all; and the smallest amount of ignorance in any matter is a bar to giving a reasonable opinion on it. However, Time works for me, and I shall be able to defend Mrs. Moxton from her enemies. Go to Goethe Cottage, Miss Gordon, and cheer Hilda."

"Do you think you can give her back her sight?"

"Perhaps! It is a difficult case. I shall have to make another examination before I can arrive at any conclusion. In the meantime, I wish her to be lively and gay; so you must realise that wish."

"Alas!" said Janet, with a melancholy smile, "I have too much experience of the world to be gay. However, I will do my best."

It will be seen from this last observation that Janet was rapidly coming under the influence of Ellis. She was a clever woman, and, in her own way, masterful; therefore, on finding someone stronger than herself, she was prepared to obey him. This sounds paradoxical, but it is so, especially in the relations of sex. A woman must always succumb to a man, if he be a man; obedience is in the feminine blood, notwithstanding the New Woman. Janet knew from experience that Ellis was kind and generous, and was willing to help to the extent of his powers those in whom he believed; now his duel with Busham--no mean adversary--had given her an impression of his strength. Moreover, she loved him, and perhaps this was why she obeyed him without a struggle. She felt the happier for such obedience, although it was new to her. When a woman finds her master in an honourable, generous, kindly man, her happiness is assured.

Therefore, Janet went to Goethe Cottage, and was welcomed by Hilda with enthusiasm. The girl was fond of her, and loved to be in such pleasant company. Warned by Schwartz, Janet was careful to avoid the theme of the murder, and indulged Hilda in the light gossip of the day, culled from society papers. She talked of literature to the girl, and read aloud to her; she played and sang, and made herself agreeable in all ways, so that Hilda became merry and happy in spite of her blindness. On the occasion of Janet's first visit, Captain Garret hung about in a nervous manner, as though he expected some catastrophe to occur. But as the sole result of Janet's presence was to make Hilda laugh, the Captain did not appear when she called again the next day. What he dreaded, Janet could not conjecture.

The second visit was merely a repetition of the first, but had in the end a far-reaching result. Hilda chattered, and sang, and talked to her birds, and fluttered about the room like a bird herself. She never made a mistake, she never stumbled or hesitated; the limits of the apartment, the disposition of the furniture, were known to her as well as though she had eyesight. Janet, watching her gyrations, could not forbear making a remark to that effect.

"Upon my word, Hilda, one would think you had eyes!"

"Oh, I know this room and my bedroom so well," chattered the blind girl. "I have been here for nearly two years, you know. But the rest of the house is like the centre of Africa to me." She paused, with a childish smile, and clapped her hands. "Let us go over it," she said.

"Certainly, if you wish. But what good will that do?"

"I want to know how the rooms are furnished. You shall take my hand, and lead me through them, describing everything that you see. Then I shall astonish Papa Schwartz and my father when they come home."

"I suppose they will have no objection?" said Janet, hesitating.

"Of course not. Papa Schwartz said that I could go anywhere so long as a friend was with me. I stay in this room because I know it from experience; and I might go wrong did I leave it. But I am not afraid to explore the house with you, dear Janet. You shall be my eyes. Come, let us start on our expedition."

Seeing no harm in this innocent proposal, Janet assented to it as a means of amusing Hilda. Hand in hand the two girls walked into the drawing-room, which Janet described in all its hideous colouring. Hilda was shocked.

"Magenta and scarlet," she said; "it sounds dreadful!"

"But you know nothing of colours, Hilda!"

"No, but my dressmaker does. And she said that magenta and scarlet were ugly. I can't imagine them myself. She saw the drawing-room, and I merely re-echoed her opinion. What is scarlet like, Janet?"

"It is a bright red."

"But what is red like?"

Janet was puzzled. She did not know how to describe the colour to one who had no conception of tint. "Red is--red," she said at length. "I can say no more. Let us go into the dining-room, Hilda."

The *salon* proved to be less glaring than the drawing-room, being papered and curtained and upholstered in dark green. The windows were few and filled with stained glass, so that the general effect was gloomy. In spite of her blindness, Hilda felt this.

"I don't like this room, it is dark," she said abruptly. "Come away, Janet."

"How do you know it is dark?" questioned Janet, as they went out.

"I cannot say. I feel happy in my own sitting-room, because I know it is bright; but here I feel wretched. I can give you no reason. But is it not curious, Janet? I can always tell dark stuff from light. I get a pain in my fingers when I touch anything black."

"Nonsense, Hilda!"

"Well, I can't describe my feelings any better to you. One has to be blind to understand these things. Where are we now, Janet?"

"In Mr. Schwartz's study. It is decorated in dark red."

"Dark again!" Hilda shuddered. "I don't like dark. Where is the desk?"

"Just before the window, where the light falls strongest."

"Lead me to it, Janet."

Janet obeyed, and Hilda ran her fingers along the top of the desk. Then she made a discovery. "Papa has left his keys," she cried. "Now, I shall open all the drawers and take away the keys, just to punish him for being careless."

"Oh, Hilda, don't do that. He might not like it."

"Yes, he will. Papa Schwartz is never angry at what I do."

"The more reason not to abuse his kindness."

"How severe you are!" cried Hilda, with a pout. "Well, I shall leave the keys, but I shall open the drawers. After all, Janet, as I am blind I cannot see his secrets."

Janet laughed, but as what Hilda said was true, she made no further opposition. While the blind girl was opening the drawers one after the other, Janet walked to the other end of the room to look at some pictures. She was recalled by a joyous laugh from Hilda, and returned to find all the drawers open. Janet took the keys from her with gentle force.

"My dear, Mr. Schwartz will not be pleased. We must close these again."

"Oh, very well," said Hilda, carelessly. "I was only joking. Close them again, Janet."

This Miss Gordon was already doing. She closed and locked the top drawers without looking much at their contents. In the bottom right-hand drawer, however, she made a discovery which amazed her. On the top of other articles she saw the red pocket-book.

CHAPTER XXIII
THE BEGINNING OF THE END

"Have you finished locking the drawers, Janet?" asked Hilda, impatiently.

But Janet did not answer. In a tumult of emotion she was staring at the red pocket-book. There it lay in the drawer, carelessly thrust in with loose papers and old letters. No attempt had been made to hide it. No doubt the drawer was locked, and but for Hilda's freak would have been opened by no one but its owner. Schwartz had not thought it necessary to conceal the book more completely. At once it flashed into Janet's mind that the German had murdered Edgar, since no one but the murderer could have become possessed of the pocket-book. In the meantime Hilda, uneasy at Janet's silence, repeated the question.

"I am just locking the last drawer," replied Janet, and, swiftly making up her mind to risk the consequences, she snatched up the red book and slipped it into her pocket. For her sister's sake it was necessary to get this evidence into her possession. Having accomplished this she locked the drawer, restored the keys to their place on the desk, and led Hilda out of the room. Towards the blind girl it was necessary to adopt a cheerful demeanour lest she should suspect that something was wrong. But Janet found this no easy task.

"Hilda, my dear," she said, as they returned to the blue sitting-room, "I have locked the drawers and replaced the keys, so Mr. Schwartz will not guess that his desk has been open. If I were you I would not tell him; he might be vexed."

The blind girl pouted. She did not like her jest to be passed over in silence.

"Papa Schwartz is never cross with me, Janet."

"No, but he will be vexed."

"Then I shall say nothing. I would not vex him for the world. He is very good to me, almost as good as father."

"You are extremely fond of your father, Hilda!"

"I worship him," said the girl, with the exaggerated emotion of youth. "He is the best man in the world. Oh, there is no one like my father."

Privately Janet thought that this was just as well, as she had no very great opinion of Captain Garret. But, bad as he was, she doubted whether he would have committed murder as Schwartz had done. It was, indeed, amazing that the German should have become a criminal; for, although Janet knew well that his character was not above reproach, yet she had always thought him a good man. It was a shock to her to find that she had been so deceived. Schwartz, who had been her good friend and benefactor, was a secret assassin. Janet could not blind herself to that terrible fact.

"Now we must have some tea," said the unsuspicious Hilda.

Under the circumstances it was an ordeal to sit at the table and eat and drink with pretended carelessness. But Janet bent her strong will to accomplish the purpose, of keeping Hilda in ignorance. The expression on her face, the frown on her brow, mattered little as Hilda was blind, but Janet carefully controlled her voice so that nothing unusual might be noticed. In this she succeeded admirably, and deceived Hilda so well that, when taking her leave, the girl had no thought that anything was wrong.

"Come again soon, dear," she said, embracing Janet warmly. "You are such a comfort to me."

Self-controlled to the end, Janet touched Hilda's cheek with her lips, and took her leave after a few words of farewell delivered in a steady voice. But on finding herself alone, she felt so anxious and distraught and horrified by her discovery, that but for the fresh air she would have fainted. As it was she did not take the Dukesfield 'bus as usual, but worked off her agitation by walking. Since the discovery of the pocket-book in Schwartz's private desk, she firmly believed that he was the criminal. In the autumn and winter he almost always wore a fur-lined coat over his evening dress, and to complete his costume, in accordance with the demands of fashion, a silk hat. Then he lived at Parkmere, and it was easy for him to walk to Goethe Cottage after committing the murder. But Janet was puzzled to find a reason for the perpetration of the crime. She knew nothing about the forged bill, as Ellis had not informed her in detail of his interview with Busham. Still, Janet knew the businesslike habits of Schwartz too well to think that he did anything without a motive, and she could not conjecture that for which he had stained his hands and risked his neck.

Full of these thoughts, Miss Gordon walked all the way to Dukesfield, no inconsiderable distance, and before seeking Myrtle Villa called on Ellis to explain her discovery. Mrs. Basket--who still believed that Janet was Mrs. Moxton--received her with the usual show of false kindness, but announced that Dr. Ellis was absent. "Though Mr. Cass is in the sitting-room," finished the fat landlady.

"Mr. Cass will do. Let me see him."

Harry was rather amazed to receive Janet, whom he had not seen--at all events, to speak to--since the night of the murder.

"Mrs. Basket announced you as Mrs. Moxton," he said, with some hesitation; "but, Ellis tells me, you are Miss Gordon?"

"Yes, I am Miss Gordon. But there is no need to let that tattling woman know the truth, she would only make mischief. Dr. Ellis is away?"

"Just went out ten minutes ago to see a patient. I expect him back in an hour."

"I cannot wait," said Janet, feverishly. "My sister will want me. You will do, Mr. Cass. Dr. Ellis informed me that you knew all about this business."

"I know everything, Miss Gordon. Anything I can do--"

"Did Dr. Ellis tell you about the red pocket-book?"

"Yes. You say it was taken from the dead body. What of it?"

Janet took the book out of her pocket and placed it on the table. "There it is," she said triumphantly. "All the papers have been taken out of it. But that is the pocket-book which the murderer stole from the corpse."

"Great Heavens! How did it come into your possession?"

"I found it by chance in the desk of Herr Schwartz."

Cass started. "Do you mean to say that Schwartz is the murderer?"

"I do. If he is not, how could he become possessed of that book?"

"It is strong circumstantial evidence certainly," said Cass, after a pause. "But Schwartz--it is incredible! I always considered him such a good fellow."

"He is, he is," said Janet, with emotion. "He has been a good friend to me. I can't conceive him guilty. Even if he is, I do not wish him punished. Let him write out a confession exonerating my sister, that is all I want."

"If he does that he puts the rope round his own neck, Miss Gordon. If your sister is to be exonerated and saved from the malignity of Busham, the confession would have to be made public."

"Then what is to be done?"

"I cannot say at present. If you will leave the pocket-book to me I will speak to Ellis, and we can come to some decision."

"Certainly I will give you the book," said Janet, rising. "I have every confidence in you and Dr. Ellis."

"Thank you. Would you mind explaining precisely how you came into possession of the pocket-book?"

"Not at all," said Janet, and she related, in a concise manner, how Hilda's prank with the desk had led to the discovery of the book.

Having given Cass all possible information, and answered all possible questions, Janet, tired out with her emotions, and with the unusual exercise, took her leave. Cass accompanied her to the door, and promised to inform her of all that should happen in connection with this new piece of evidence. Somewhat relieved, Janet went home to Myrtle Villa.

Immediately on the doctor's return, Cass showed him the pocket-book, and repeated Janet's story. Ellis, naturally enough, was as surprised as his friend, and discussed the matter with him at length. Finally, it was decided that Ellis should see Schwartz that same evening, and hear what he had to say for himself. Owing to the exigencies of his profession as critic, Harry could not accompany his friend. The doctor was not sorry, as he thought that he could get more out of Schwartz when alone with him than in the presence of a third person. He did not take the pocket-book with him lest it should be lost, for Schwartz was a determined man to deal with. As yet Ellis could hardly credit that he was guilty, and in spite of the damning evidence found by Janet he postponed, making up his mind until he heard what the German had to say for himself. In this frame of mind he started for the Merryman Music-Hail.

Schwartz was in his private room, and as Ellis had purposely arrived rather late he was at leisure at the time. So effusively did he welcome Ellis that the doctor felt almost ashamed of his errand, but, bracing himself up with the idea that Schwartz, if not the actual criminal, yet knew something about the crime, he managed to appear sufficiently stern. To the German's eager inquiries about Hilda's health and Hilda's eyesight he gave brief and monosyllabic replies. At last Schwartz was forced to take notice of his visitor's unfriendly attitude.

"What is not right, doctor?" he asked anxiously.

Ellis glanced round to see that the door was closed, and cleared his throat.

"Mr. Schwartz," he said in low tones, "I have come to see you about a very unpleasant business."

The German turned paler even than he was, and his hand shook as he tried to light a cigar. "Ach! Is dat zo?"

"It is about Moxton's murder."

"Veil, veil, what apout ze murder?" queried Schwartz, impatiently.

"I should rather put that question to you, Schwartz. Why was Moxton murdered--or rather, why was he got out of the way?"

Instead of answering his question, Schwartz, in a tremor of nervous excitement, rose and locked the door. "Can you speak German?" he asked, in his own tongue, on returning to his seat.

"A little. I can speak it slowly."

"Then put your questions in that language," said Schwartz, savagely. "I can see that you have come to accuse me of being mixed up in this crime. Was it for this purpose that you called at my house?"

"You forget. I called, at your request, to see Miss Garret."

Schwartz sighed. "Ach! the liddle Hilda," he said in English; then slipping back into his own tongue, he demanded what Ellis wished to know.

"I wish to know if you can tell me the reason Moxton was murdered?" said Ellis, slowly, in German.

"No, I cannot. I know nothing about it."

"Then I must tell you--that is, I must refresh your memory. Moxton was murdered by a man who wished to obtain possession of a forged bill."

The German bit his cigar through, and a portion fell on the floor. "I know nothing of any forged bill," he said angrily.

"That bill," resumed Ellis, calmly, "was placed by Moxton in a red pocket-book." Here Schwartz started and groaned. "Zirknitz saw him put it there. When the clothes of the corpse were examined, that pocket-book was missing; and, strange to say, Mr. Schwartz, it was found to-day in your desk at Goethe Cottage."

"In my desk!" gasped the man. "Who--who found it there?"

"Miss Gordon. For a jest, Miss Garret opened all the drawers of your desk, because you were foolish enough to leave your keys behind. Miss Gordon closed them again. In the lowest drawer she saw and recognised the pocket-book of her brother-in-law. That book is now in her possession-- or rather, in mine, as she gave it to me."

There was silence for a few moments, and Schwartz breathed heavily. "What do you want me to do?" he said sullenly.

"Confess your guilt."

"And if I do--what then?"

"Then you must write out and sign a confession as to how you killed Edgar Moxton, and why."

"To hang myself, I suppose?" said Schwartz, who was growing alarmingly red in the face.

"No; Miss Gordon is too much indebted to you to wish for your death. Write the confession, and then fly from England. Thus Mrs. Moxton will be exonerated, and you will be safe."

"Ach! it is goot of Chanet," said Schwartz, thickly; "it is--it is--ah--ah!" He tried to rise from his seat, but suddenly gave a choking cry, and fell back, purple in the face, with staring eyes and foam on his lips.

Ellis rapidly unloosened the old man's cravat, tore off his collar, and threw open the door.

"Come here, someone," he cried. "Herr Schwartz is in a fit!"

CHAPTER XXIV
THE TRUTH

When Schwartz recovered from the fit, he was taken home in a cab, and for the time being Ellis saw no more of him. He was really puzzled how to act, for the man was evidently guilty, as he had not denied the crime. For the sake of Janet, who had received benefits at the hands of Schwartz, the doctor did not wish to denounce him to the police. If he left behind him a written confession exonerating Mrs. Moxton, Ellis was quite content that he should seek safety in flight. Certainly he had murdered a man, and although his victim was a worthless scoundrel, still there was no excuse to be made for so heinous a crime. But would hanging Schwartz do any good? Ellis thought not, neither did Cass, nor Janet.

"If it was Busham," said Harry, "I would see him swing with the greatest pleasure, for he is a thoroughly bad lot; but Schwartz has so many good qualities that I should like to give him a chance of repentance."

"And the crime was not committed deliberately," chimed in Janet. "I feel sure that Mr. Schwartz did not come to Dukesfield with the intention of murdering Edgar. No doubt he wanted that forged bill, and hoped to rob Edgar while he was drunk. It was seeing the carving-knife in Laura's hand which made him a criminal. Temptation was put in his way, and he snatched at it almost without thinking. Under these circumstances, and because he has been kind to me, I should like him to escape."

"He can take his own chance of that," said Ellis; "but to counter-plot Busham, it is necessary to get a full confession from Schwartz."

"But he may go away without making any confession, Bob!"

"I don't think so. Not until he is in absolute peril of his life will he leave his idol, Hilda. Besides, I called at Goethe Cottage, and he is still ill after his fit."

"Did you see him, doctor?"

"No, he refused to see me, being engaged with Garret. But I saw Hilda, and she is lamenting your absence, Miss Gordon."

"I cannot go round to the cottage now," said Janet, with a mournful shake of her head. "Mr. Schwartz thinks that I have been a spy and ungrateful."

"Indeed you wrong him," said Ellis, quickly. "He was much touched when I told him that you did not wish the police to be told. He would have said more about it, only he fell into the fit."

This conversation took place in Ellis's sitting-room on the evening of the day following Janet's discovery of the pocket-book. Schwartz was still ill, and, as Ellis said, would see no one. The three--Cass, Ellis and Janet--were now anxiously discussing what was best to be done. They wanted to thwart Busham, to save Mrs. Moxton and to spare Schwartz; but none of these three things were easy to do. Since Ellis had given his ultimatum to the lawyer, nothing had been heard from Esher Lane. Janet was inclined to think that Busham, afraid of being implicated in the crime, had fled; but Cass and Ellis were satisfied that the man, with his grasping, foxy, intriguing nature, would stay and face the matter until his personal safety was compromised. While they were discussing this point, the door opened abruptly, and Busham himself entered the room. It was a case of "Talk of the Devil and you will see his hoof." The trio were completely taken by surprise at his unlooked-for appearance and his insolent entry.

"He! he!" sniggered Busham, who had all his natural impudence about him. "I just looked in to see Dr. Ellis, and I find company. How do you do, Miss Gordon, or Mrs. Moxton--which?"

"I am Janet Gordon, Mr. Busham! I think you know that."

"Indeed, I do not, dear lady. You are one of twins, remember--a kind of double-face female, Janus, eh?"

"Cease your insolence, man!" said Ellis, angrily, "and tell me how dare you walk into my room without knocking?"

"Oh, I informed your landlady that I was an old friend of yours, so she let me pass. She looks a fool, doctor. You don't offer me a seat. Well, I will anticipate your hospitality and take one. And who is this gentleman?"

"My name is Cass. I am a journalist," said Harry, enraged at the man's impudence. "What the deuce do you come here for?"

"Not to see you, my dear sir. My business is with Dr. Ellis, and possibly with Miss Gordon."

"Have you come to confess?" asked Janet, quietly.

"Confess! I have nothing to confess. I come here to make a proposal."

Ellis shrugged his shoulders. "You have brass enough for anything, I think," said he. "Well, Mr. Busham, and what is your proposal?"

"Let Mrs. Moxton surrender all my uncle's property to me. Now that Edgar is dead, I am his rightful heir, being his nephew, and nearest of kin. I destroyed the will--I don't mind admitting it, because Mrs. Moxton is in my power, and it is my place to make terms, not to be dictated to. Well, then, as the will is burnt, I take a portion of the property as next-of-kin; but that will not satisfy me. I want the whole, and," cried Busham, in a threatening tone, "I mean to have it!"

"What a modest demand," jeered Cass. "And if Mrs. Moxton surrenders her property as you wish, what then?"

"I shall tell you who killed Moxton. Oh, you need not look at me as though I was an accessory before the fact. I did not see the deed done. I knew nothing about it at the time, but by putting this and that together in a way," sneered Busham, "which you are all too ignorant to understand, I have a knowledge of who killed Edgar, and why he was killed. Don't mistake me. I hold all the threads of this case. If I get my price I shall save Mrs. Moxton by revealing the name of the murderer. Should she refuse my just demand, I shall denounce her to the police and let justice take its course."

"Justice!" echoed Janet, with scorn. "And by your own showing my unhappy sister is innocent."

"I know that," retorted Busham, with an ugly look, "and I can prove her innocence. No one else can."

There was a silence for a few minutes, and then Ellis spoke quietly and to the point. "Do you know, Busham, that I feel very much inclined to kick you," said he. "You are proposing blackmail."

"Call it what you like, but give me my price."

"For what? For information which we know already?"

Busham started from his seat in nervous haste. "You know already!"

"Yes. Do you think Mr. Cass and I have been idle all this time--that we have not strained every nerve to baffle a scoundrel like you, and protect two innocent women from your blackmail? You are a little late, Mr. Busham. We know who killed Moxton."

"You--you--you know!" stammered the scoundrel, white to the lips.

"Yes, we know; and we have discovered the reason why Moxton was killed. Surely you have forgotten our talk about the forged bill. Before the end of the present week the murderer will have confessed, Mrs. Moxton will be exonerated from all complicity in her husband's death, and you, Mr. Busham--well, I don't know about you. But from what I guess of your share in this tragedy, you will be in gaol."

"I had nothing to do with it. Who killed Moxton?"

"Oh," laughed Cass, delighted at the confusion of Busham, "as you know there is no need to tell you the name."

The baffled lawyer looked in turn at each of the scornful faces. Then he rose in a hurry. "This is a game of bluff," he cried savagely. "You do not know who murdered Edgar, and you are trying to get my secret from me without paying for it. Oh, I know you all; I can see through you."

"It does you credit," said Janet, contemptuously.

"Sneer and jeer as much as you like, madam, you will not look so merry when your sister is in prison on a charge of murder."

"Which she never will be," put in Ellis.

"We shall see, we shall see. You think yourself a clever man, doctor, do you not? But I am cleverer. Oh, you don't know what I am. You gave me five days to confess, as you call it, or else threatened to put the matter into the hands of the police. The five days are up."

"Quite so," said Ellis, smoothly, "and as you won't hear reason I shall see the police to-morrow."

"I dare you to! I dare you to!" foamed Busham, who had completely lost his temper. "I get my price, or Mrs. Moxton goes to gaol."

"You shall not get your price," broke out Cass, as furious as Busham. "You will not get one penny of the property."

"Shall I not? Aha, you don't know that Edgar's will is burnt."

"That is where you are wrong, my friend," said Ellis, calmly. "You burnt a copy. The original will given to me by Miss Gordon is in my possession."

Busham stared so wildly that for a moment or so the others thought he was about to have a fit like Schwartz. Ellis snatched up a glass of water from the table and dashed it in the man's face. The shock brought him round a trifle, but he seemed indisposed to speak further. With the knowledge that his intrigues had proved useless came a collapse of his courage and insolence. With a kind of sob he staggered blindly towards the door and out of the room. Ellis at the window saw him running down the road, reeling from side to side like a drunken man. Busham's nerve was broken. He did not even attempt to question Ellis as to the truth of his statement about the will. Instinctively he knew that the game was up, and that all his schemes had recoiled on himself. Never was there so complete a fall, so deserved a punishment.

"He will tell the police about Laura," cried Miss Gordon, nervously.

"Let him," said Cass. "We will have that confession out of Schwartz to-morrow, and your sister will be proved innocent; and when that confession is read, Miss Gordon, I should not wonder if there was sufficient in it to warrant Busham's arrest. There," added Cass, pointing to Busham's disappearing form, "that is the last we shall see of him." And, as subsequent events proved, he was a true prophet.

But the danger was not yet over. It was just possible that out of revenge at the failure of his plans, Busham might denounce Laura to the police. The only way to prove her innocence would be to get a confession from Schwartz. Ellis took the night to consider this question, and next day called at Goethe Cottage between eleven and twelve o'clock. He sent in his name, but quite expected that Schwartz would refuse to see him. To his secret surprise he was admitted at once and conducted into the study. Here he found the German clothed in a loose dressing-gown and seated at the desk.

Schwartz looked terribly ill. He had aged considerably since Ellis had seen him. His cheeks had fallen in, his forehead was wrinkled, and his eyes had lost their usual genial twinkle. With bowed shoulders he sat huddled up in his chair, and without offering his hand to the doctor, nodded to a seat.

"I am sorry I could not see you yesterday, doctor," said Schwartz, in a faint voice; "I was very ill, and I had much to do. But I wished to have some conversation with you to-day. If you had not come I should have sent for you."

Ellis replied in the German tongue which Schwartz, evidently for the sake of secrecy, was using. "You intend to confess, then?"

"Ah, then you are certain that I am guilty?"

"You must be. The pocket-book of the murdered man was found in that desk, and we know it was taken from the dead body. The other night when I accused you, you did not deny the charge."

"I had no time, doctor; but I deny it now."

"You say that you are innocent?" said Ellis, scarcely believing his ears.

"Perfectly innocent. Here is the confession of the guilty person;" and Schwartz, unlocking a drawer, took out two or three sheets of foolscap pinned together and covered with writing. "This is the confession," he said, "signed and witnessed."

"The confession of Busham?"

"Ach, no; the confession of the man who murdered Moxton--my friend, Hilda's father, Captain Garret."

CHAPTER XXV
A CONFESSION

"Do you mean to say that Captain Garret murdered Moxton?" asked Ellis, in amazement, looking from the confession to Schwartz. In his excitement he had reverted to English.

"Hush! hush!" replied Schwartz, with an apprehensive look round. "Speak in my language, doctor. Yes, Garret is the criminal. I have known it for some time, ever since I found the pocket-book, and yesterday, on seeing in what a very dangerous position I was placed, I insisted that he should write out a confession of the truth. There it is, doctor; and a great deal of money it has cost me."

"And Garret. Where is Garret?"

"On the Continent by this time. He left Victoria by the club train last night. I have seen the last of him," said Schwartz, with a sigh, "and I am glad of it."

"But Hilda?"

"Ach, poor girl! She thinks that her father has gone away for pleasure. I dare not tell her the truth; but in time I may do so, and then she will be content to stay with old Papa Schwartz who loves her."

"It is most extraordinary," murmured Ellis, turning over the leaves of foolscap. "I suspected many people, yourself included, but I never thought for a moment that Garret was guilty. How did it come about?"

"To tell you that, doctor, I must relate a little of my own history," said Schwartz, reaching for the cigar-box. "First I will tell you about myself and Garret, and then you can read what he says of the crime in that paper. Will you not take a cigar?"

"Thank you," said Ellis, and accepted this attention.

Now that he knew Schwartz was innocent he had no objection to being friendly with him; indeed, he was pleased to think that the German was guiltless, as he ever thought the man a decent fellow in many ways. They began to smoke, and Schwartz, still speaking in German in case of eavesdropping, related such portions of his early history as dealt with Captain Garret and his daughter.

"Ten years ago I met with Garret near Monte Carlo," said Schwartz. "His wife had died, and he wandered about with little Hilda, then only six years old. Garret had started life as an officer in your army with money and a well-known name, for that which he bears now is not his true name. He married an heiress and for years was comfortably settled. Unfortunately, he took to gambling and lost everything. Having been discovered cheating at cards he was dismissed from your army. Then his wife died, and his house was sold up to pay his debts. He took the child and escaped to the Continent. But his love of gambling still clung to him. He took up his quarters in a cheap boarding-house in Monaco, and haunted the tables. The child Hilda, blind and helpless, was left to a careless nurse. I was hard up myself then, doctor, and also lived in that boarding-house. I saw Hilda, and my heart melted. She was a dear little child, and became fond of me, so that, in time, I came to look upon her as my own daughter."

"You are a good fellow, Schwartz."

"Ach, no, my friend, I am as bad as most people. But I never married, I was a lonely man with much sentiment and emotion. Hilda loved me, she warmed my heart. I saw that she was neglected by her father, and I determined to look after her, poor dear, to make her happy."

"I think you have succeeded."

"I think so too. Yet she loves her father better than me. He was never kind to her, save in a careless way. It is always so. Hilda thinks Garret the best of men, and I have not the heart to tell her how worthless he is. Believe me, my friend, I was never blind to Garret's badness. What I did for him, I did for the little Hilda's sake. Garret met me at the boarding-house and told me his history. I offered to give him money if he would let me adopt Hilda, but seeing that my heart was touched he cunningly refused. I could not part with the child, so I had to take the burden of Garret's life on my shoulders. I said that I would help him and look after him if he was kind to little Hilda. He consented, and we have been together ever since."

"Did Garret ever make any money?"

"No, he was always idle and wasted everything. Sometimes he won money and spent it on himself; but I had to keep both him and Hilda. It was for her sake that I did so, for otherwise Garret would have taken her away from me; and that," added Schwartz, with emotion, "would have broken my heart."

"Why did you not tell Hilda all this?"

"Why should I have done so?" replied the good German, with great simplicity. "It would have broken the child's heart. It would spoil her life did I tell her now. Poor Hilda! She has enough to bear without my making her wretched. It is my wish that she should be happy. She is the dearest thing on earth to me. Without that lovely child I should die."

"I am glad you have some comfort and reward," said Ellis, touched by this speech. "So Garret, through Hilda, has lived on your money all these years?"

"Yes. Oh, I was quite willing so long as he left me the child. I need not tell you all the troubles I have had these many years, doctor. I made money, I lost money. I was poor one year, rich another; but all through my fortunes Hilda has been with me--Garret also. Three years ago I came to London, and after several failures I started the Merryman Music-Hall. It has been a success, and now I am rich. I have settled much money on Hilda, also this cottage. Even if I die she will be well off."

"If you died, her father would return and rob her."

"I often dreaded that, but now my fears are at rest. While this confession remains with you, doctor, I am not afraid. Garret admits that he is a murderer, so for his own sake he will never return to England. Now I have told you all I know about Garret, which brings us up to the time of the murder. The rest you can read in those papers."

"I shall do so later," replied Ellis, glancing at the confession, and putting it into his pocket. "But you might tell me the story in your own way. What was the reason of the tragedy?"

"The forged bill you spoke of the other night."

"Who forged the bill?"

"Garret. I refused to give him any more money as he was squandering all I had. He was acquainted with young Moxton, and knew how rich the elder Moxton was. Edgar showed Garret a letter from his father, so Garret forged the old man's signature on a bill. He accepted it himself, and managed to get money on it. Of course, he thought that if he were discovered I would buy back the bill at any price, so that he would not be disgraced. He counted on my love for Hilda, you see."

"And how was the forgery discovered?"

"Old Moxton found it out just before he died. He passed the bill on to Busham, as his lawyer, to take steps to arrest Garret. Busham did not do anything at the moment. Then old Moxton died, and that same night Busham brought the bill to Edgar at my music-hall."

"Ah! then in spite of his denial he met Edgar on that night?"

"Garret told me so," replied Schwartz. "I knew very little of Edgar Moxton save that he was a bad man. Busham gave him the bill, for Edgar, on hearing of his father's death, insisted upon having it."

"How did he know that the bill was in existence?"

"Busham told him about it, when Edgar inquired after the estates. He did not care at all about his father's death. He wanted the money; and although he was now rich he still wished for more. Janet Gordon had told him how I looked after Garret on Hilda's account, and he knew, of course, that the music-hall was my property. He then followed Garret into my room where I was, and, showing him the bill, accused him of the forgery. I saw him replace the bill in the red pocket-book and put that in his pocket. Garret also saw in which pocket he placed it."

"What did Moxton want?"

"The music-hall. He had been drinking, and was also intoxicated by the money that had come to him. He said that if I did not give him the music-hall and make it over legally to him, he would have Garret arrested."

"What did you do? How did you answer the scoundrel?" asked Ellis.

"I refused," replied Schwartz, with energy. "I had done much for Garret, but even for Hilda's sake I could not beggar her and myself by giving up my property. Garret insisted that I should save him at any cost, but I said I could do nothing; and Moxton went away swearing that he would have Garret arrested on the morrow."

"And Garret?"

"Finding that I would do nothing he rushed away distracted. What I now tell you he told me afterwards. By accident he took my fur-lined coat and put it on, leaving his own behind. Then he followed Edgar home in the hope of robbing him of the bill while he was drunk. He saw Zirknitz quarrel with Edgar on the Dukesfield platform and kept out of the way. Then he followed Moxton when he left the station."

"Busham followed also?"

"Yes, but he did not let Garret see him. Busham wished to get back the bill himself, as he wanted to keep all power in his own hands. That was why he followed Edgar from the music-hall. On seeing Garret, he wondered what he was after, and watched."

"Oh," said Ellis, "so this was what Busham did? His talk with the policeman and pursuit of Mrs. Moxton to Pimlico was all lies."

"I don't know about those things, doctor. Garret followed Edgar to the gate of Myrtle Villa, when he saw the door open, and Mrs. Moxton rush out with a carving-knife. Moxton began to struggle with her at the gate. She held the knife over him--I don't know why."

"She did not wish to hurt him. Go on."

"Garret saw the knife flash in the moonlight, so he ran along, and seizing it, stabbed Moxton in the back. He fell with a cry and Mrs. Moxton under him. Garret ran away, but returned to find Edgar dead, and Mrs. Moxton in a faint."

"That must have been the time when Edgar wrote the blood-signs."

"Yes, no doubt. Well, Garret searched for the pocket-book and found it. He threw the knife beside the corpse, thinking it would be said that Mrs. Moxton had killed her husband. Then, hearing footsteps approaching, he went away quickly."

"That must have been Miss Gordon. She returned for her purse, and on finding what had happened, remained to shield her sister. Brave woman!"

"Ach! my friend, that is so. Janet is both brave and good. But to continue, Garret went into a quiet part of Dukesfield and took the bill out of the pocket-book. As he was burning it--for he destroyed it at once by setting light to it with a match--Busham came up and accused him of the murder."

"Did Busham see it committed?"

"He did. He followed Garret, and, hidden in the shade, saw him stab Moxton. But he promised to hold his tongue about it, provided he got Moxton's money. Garret was relieved by this promise, and putting the pocket-book into the pocket of my coat, which he wore, he returned to Goethe Cottage."

"To confess his crime?"

"No, he said nothing; and even though I heard of Edgar's death, I did not think that Garrett had killed him. But when I put on my coat one evening I found the pocket-book, and recognised it as Edgar's. I then accused Garret of the murder, and he told me all I have told you. I held my tongue, for Hilda's sake, and as Busham was hoping to get the money by accusing Mrs. Moxton of the crime, he was silent too. I placed the pocket-book in my desk, where Janet found it. I should have destroyed it, but I thought no one would open my desk. Hilda, by her folly, has ruined her father, but I shall not make her heart ache by telling her so."

"What did you say to Garret?"

"I told him that you had the pocket-book, and accused me of the crime. I refused to suffer for his sake, and made him write out the confession, which is witnessed by myself and two servants. But they do not know the contents. I threatened to hand Garret over to the police if he did not tell the truth, as I wished to save myself and Hilda. Then I gave him some money, and told him to go away and never let me see him again. He wanted to take Hilda, but I gave him the choice of leaving her with me, or suffering for his crime. In the end, he went away last night, and so that is all I can tell you."

"I think you are well rid of a bad lot, Herr Schwartz."

"I think so too," replied the German. "I never liked him; but for the sake of Hilda I tolerated him. I will not tell her the truth; but as Garret is away, and will remain away, I have no doubt I can explain sufficient to reconcile her to his absence. So I have my Hilda to myself at last, doctor, and thank God for that."

CHAPTER XXVI
THE END OF THE STORY

So in this way the truth was discovered, and Ellis returned to show the confession of Captain Garret to Mrs. Moxton. Laura was so overcome that her innocence was proved, her dread was removed, that she fainted during the recital. While Ellis and Janet were looking after her, Cass arrived. Mrs. Moxton recovered her senses, and retired to lie down; while Harry, having read the confession, discussed what was to be done with it.

"If you show it to the police, I am afraid Schwartz will get into trouble, as he has permitted a criminal to escape."

"That is true enough," replied Ellis. "For my part, now that we have absolute proof of Mrs. Moxton's innocence, I don't think it is necessary to make the matter public."

"Mr. Busham may do so, out of revenge," said Janet.

"Don't you believe it, Miss Gordon. Busham, by the showing of this confession, knew all about the crime. He saw it committed, he tampered with Garret, and held his tongue in order to secure Moxton's money. On the face of it, he is an accessory after the fact, and, terrified by the fear of punishment, will keep silence. Besides, even if he does speak, we can first warn Schwartz to leave England, and then inform the police. Busham does not know, and never will know, that Schwartz has been implicated in Garret's escape."

"What Harry says is very true," chimed in Ellis. "I think all danger is over."

"Thank God for that!" cried Janet, clasping her hands. "Oh, how terrible these past months have been!"

"You will have no more trouble if I can help it," said the doctor, taking her hand. "What I said when I believed you to be Mrs. Moxton, I say now; and I ask you to be my honoured wife."

Janet sobbed. "You forget! I have a shady past!"

"A noble past. You have been tested in the furnace of affliction, and have come out pure gold."

"I sold programmes at a low music-hall."

"My dearest, I know all you have done, and how good you have been. As my wife, I hope you will find that happiness which has been denied to you for so long. You love me, Janet, do you not?"

"Yes, I love you, because you believed in me when no one else did."

Harry laughed in a somewhat shamefaced manner. "Is that meant for me, Miss Gordon? If so, I recant my former errors. I think you are the noblest of women, and I congratulate Bob on getting such a wife."

"Hullo! Harry. I thought you did not want me to marry Janet."

"Now I do, because I know the truth. Bless you, my children, and let me be your best man."

"There is one thing to be said," observed Ellis, uneasily. "Janet cannot marry me here, where she is known as Mrs. Moxton. Mrs. Basket may make trouble, and I cannot afford to give up my practice--such as it is."

"Leave that to me," said Janet, nodding. "My sister Laura owes you everything, and when she gets her fortune she will give you enough money to buy a practice far away from Mrs. Basket and this horrid little place. I am sure I do not wish to live in this district after what I have undergone. When I leave Myrtle Villa, I leave Dukesfield for ever."

"But, Janet, I don't like taking money from Mrs. Moxton."

"Why not? Because it is red money?"

"Red money!" repeated Cass, struck by the phrase, "and what is red money?"

"Ah!" said Janet, smiling, "then there is something you don't know of which I am aware. Red money is a term given by gipsies to that which comes by a violent death. My sister inherits her fortune through the murder of her husband; therefore, according to Romany lore, it is red money. But if Robert will not take the money from Laura, she shall give it to me. She owes me something, I think."

"She owes you everything, my dearest," said Ellis, kissing her, "and you will do what you please."

"Oh, by the way," cried Cass, suddenly, "I thought I had something to tell you. Schwartz has given up his secret gambling *salon*."

"Did it ever exist?" said Ellis, sceptically.

"Yes," replied Janet, blushing. "I never saw it, but in one way and another I heard of it. Often and often I implored Papa Schwartz to give it up, telling him he would get into trouble."

"Well, he has given it up at last. It appears that the police got to know of it, and contemplated a raid, so Schwartz shut it up a few nights ago; and I rather think he is going to give up the hall itself."

"A very wise thing for him to do," said Ellis, approvingly. "He has made a sufficient fortune--he told me so; therefore he can retire and live happily with his beloved Hilda."

"And what about Hilda's eyes, Robert?"

"I think I can cure them by an operation."

"Oh, I am sure you can do anything," said Janet, fervently.

But in this Janet was wrong. Ellis did perform an operation, but it failed principally because Hilda, fretting after her father, could not be kept in a serene frame of mind during the recovery. But the cure mattered little, for shortly there came news from Madrid that Garret had been stabbed in a gambling-house row. By the irony of fate he met with the same death as he had meted out to Moxton, and Hilda wept so much that her chance of recovering sight was irrevocably gone. On hearing of Garret's death, and being set free from a dread that Hilda would be taken from him, Schwartz went to reside in Munich. He sold the music-hall and the cottage, invested his money well, and with Hilda he now lives a calm and happy life in the German Athens; and in spite of his late business of a gambling-house keeper and the many flaws in his character, Schwartz deserved to be happy. He rescued the blind girl from a life of misery; he bore the burdens of her rascally father, and he made her happy. Under the tender care of Schwartz, Hilda forgot her sorrow. She never knew that her father was a murderer, and always thought of him with tender affection as the best and most unfortunate of men. Schwartz did not disturb this impression, knowing that Garret was not the first sinner who had been wrongly canonised as a saint. All the good German desired was the happiness of his beloved Hilda, and in securing it he thoroughly succeeded. That was his reward, and so he passes out of the story.

Janet never did have much belief in Laura's gratitude, and said as much to Ellis. Her belief came true, for when Laura, relieved from her terrors, blossomed into a wealthy young widow on her father-in-law's money, she forgot all that her sister had done and sacrificed for her. It was no easy task to settle the estate, for, when Busham was informed by letter that Garret had confessed, he was seized with panic and went to the States.

But he did not go away empty-handed; that was not Mr. Busham's way of doing things. Already he had ample money, but he managed also to secure a good deal of loose cash which belonged to the Moxton estate, and left behind him an insulting letter to Ellis. In America, Busham changed his name, but as wickedness was born in him he could not change his nature. What became of him Ellis never heard. He vanished into the vast unknown of the States; but, having regard to the money he took with him and his known capabilities of screwing it out of others, it is quite possible that he is flourishing at present like a green bay tree. The wicked are not always punished in this world, and Busham's escape is an illustration of this fact. Still, his inherent rascality may some day bring him before Mr. Justice Lynch, and he may end as he deserves.

Dr. Ellis worked loyally to put Mrs. Moxton's affairs in order, and received from her the same gratitude as she gave to Janet. For very shame's sake she was obliged to give her sister a sum of money in compensation for all she had done. Ellis did not wish to take a sum so grudgingly given, but Janet looked upon it as her right, and took it without false shame. She was as disgusted with Laura as with Rudolph, and was glad to see the last of them. All her years of self-sacrifice and work were as nothing in their eyes, and now that Janet had found a good husband she thought it was only right to look after her own happiness. A few months after the discovery of Garret's guilt she was married quietly to Ellis in a Hampstead church, and afterwards departed with him to a country town, where Ellis, with Mrs. Moxton's money, bought a practice. Neither Laura nor Rudolph came to the wedding, as they had already gone to the Continent. After he had confessed his traitorous behaviour, Rudolph called on Janet and tried to cajole her into forgiving him. But she was so disgusted with him that she refused to have anything more to do with the rascal. He was more successful with Laura, and as she was now rich, he paid great attention to her. Notwithstanding her knowledge of his contemptible character, Laura went abroad with him and kept him in idleness with her wealth. The pair travelled to Vienna and there lived as happily as a memory of the terrible past would let them. This means that they had not a care in the world, for both their natures were too frivolous to be impressed by the perils they had escaped. So, like Busham, they flourished also, and deserved their immunity from punishment as little.

Mrs. Basket lamented bitterly when she lost her lodger, and tried to find out why and where he was going. But Ellis, having had experience of his fat landlady's malignity, refused to gratify her curiosity. Also he wished to cut himself and Janet off from the old life of trouble at Dukesfield, and so vanished from Mrs. Basket's gaze. Cass remained with her for a time, but as his circumstances improved, he decided to move into town, and took chambers in St. Clement's Inn. In this way and in a few years all the actors in the Moxton tragedy disappeared from Dukesfield, and no reminder was left of it but the tombstone erected over the wretched man's grave by Laura. The inscription, "Erected by his sorrowful wife," was rather ironical, when it was considered how Laura hated the man she thus honoured. But Laura was fond of posing as a disconsolate widow. She thought it attracted the men.

A year after the tragedy Harry Cass paid a visit to the country town where Ellis lived, and in which his practice was rapidly increasing. He possessed a charming house on the outskirts of the old town; he had set up a carriage, and possessed a good hack. Aided by Janet's good sense and strict notions of an economy instilled by poverty, the sum of money grudgingly given by Laura had done wonders, and Dr. Ellis started his new life on an excellent basis. He was not a great physician, but he was clever and also popular. The ladies in the neighbourhood called on Mrs. Ellis and found her charming, for Janet's life, and travels, and experience led her to adapt herself skilfully to the provincial narrowness of these good people. She was quite as popular as her husband, and in time there is no doubt that Ellis will become the most sought-after physician in the county.

"But Harley Street, Bob," urged Harry, as he sat with husband and wife in the garden after dinner. "What about Harley Street?"

"That must wait," laughed Ellis; "and if it does not come I really don't care. Do you remember my expressed wishes, Harry, on the night Moxton was killed? 'A good practice, a moderate income, a home, and a wife to love me.' Well, I have got the whole four, and that is better luck than falls to the lot of most men. I am quite content to stay here and be happy."

"And you, Mrs. Ellis, after your stormy, early life?"

"I am content to remain in this haven," smiled Janet. "I have a good home and a loving husband. What more can a woman want?" "Egad! some women want a sight more. Your story is not known here?"

"No," replied Ellis, promptly. "Janet and I have cut ourselves off completely from the past. We never think of it."

"Except when we are obliged," said Mrs. Ellis. "I received a letter from Laura the other day. She is going to be married to an Austrian officer, a young Count who is deeply in love with her."

"H'm! or with her money?" said Cass. "However, if she buys a title in that way I suppose she will be satisfied. And her husband has only been dead a year! She is soon consoled. I hope she will have better luck with her second husband than she had with her first. And Zirknitz?"

"He is in Italy, in attendance on an American heiress."

"Oh, poor heiress! He will marry her and spend her money."

"Laura says nothing about marriage."

"But it will take place all the same," said Cass, promptly. "Zirknitz is the most fascinating scoundrel I ever met. Even though a woman knew he was a scamp she would love him. Oh, he'll marry money and be rich, and, having no heart, be as happy as the day is long."

"Well, Edgar never liked him."

"I know that, else he would not have accused him of being his murderer."

"As to that," said Ellis, musingly, "I can never quite understand Moxton's reason. If he did not wish to harm Zirknitz, why did he write the initials of his name at all? If he did, why put them in a secret writing known only to his wife and Janet?"

Janet shook her head. "I think at the last he had some compunction for the way in which he had treated Laura. He believed that Zirknitz had killed him, and wished to give Laura power over him lest he should take her money."

"That is not a very satisfactory explanation," said Cass, with a shrug. "But I suppose no other can be given. At all events, Zirknitz did get some of Laura's money."

"Red money," said Mrs. Ellis, with a shudder; "the money of violence!"

"Well, red money has done a lot for me," said the doctor, putting his arm round his wife's waist; "it has given me this ease and you."

"Not me, Robert. I came to you of my own accord."

"Dearest and best of women," said Ellis, and kissed her fondly.